DECEPTION

DECEPTION

Isabelle Van Buren

This is a work of fiction. Names, characters, businesses, places, events, and incidents are either the products of the author's imagination or used in a fictitious manner. Any resemblance to actual persons, living or dead, or actual events is purely coincidental.

Copyright © 2015 Isabelle Van Buren

All rights reserved. No part of this publication may be reproduced, distributed, or transmitted in any form or by any means, including photocopying, recording, or other electronic or mechanical methods, without the prior written permission of the publisher except for the use of brief quotations in a book review.

Printed in the United States of America

ISBN-13: 978-1546491378
ISBN-10: 1546491376

This book is dedicated to my sister, Evelyn

chapter ONE

Friday
April 12, 2013
10:04 a.m.

Sauntering out of the courtroom, I press two on my cell phone, but when it starts to ring, I press End. Tears well in my eyes. Far too often over the past three hundred thirty-six days, I've forgotten that I can no longer call my dad as I once did. I press three and wait for my mom to answer.

"I did it," I shout into the phone, over the loud chanting and chatter in the background.

"Oh honey, I knew you would. Your dad would be so proud."

Yes, my dad would be proud. My dad was always proud of me but knowing that I won the biggest case of my career in just under a year of taking over his law firm would have certainly put tears of joy in his eyes. That thought puts tears in my eyes.

After telling her that I'll call with more details once I get back to the office, we hang up. Feeling a hand on my shoulder, I turn around to find my client, Kelly.

"Thank you again, Amy," she says with tears streaming down her face. I hug her.

"You're welcome, but you deserve this."

Kelly was accused of killing her five-year-old son. It was a long, drawn-out trial that stretched over four weeks. But in the end, there was no denying she would have never done such an unspeakable act to her child. Every single piece of evidence proved Kelly had nothing to do with the murder. But her monstrous ex-husband sure did. Now she gets to go home to her other son, who was temporarily taken into custody by the state.

When we pull away from our hug, I hear a little voice from within the mass of reporters. "Mommy!" Evan, Kelly's seven-year-old son, bolts in our direction.

I squeeze Kelly's hand. "Go to your son and finally start healing."

After walking into a sea of flashing cameras and questions, I step outside the courthouse. I draw in a deep breath, pushing my way down the stairs to the town car awaiting me.

"Surprise!"

I open the door to the law firm and the room explodes in cheers. Quickly scanning the room, I see all my colleagues, as well as my mom, sister, and brother. My heart starts to find its rhythm again as Laura, my long-time best friend and an attorney at the firm, meets me with a glass of champagne.

"Congratulations, Amy. We know that winning this case was one of the most important things in your life. We're so proud of you."

While I knew since the age of four that I wanted to be a lawyer someday, I also knew that I had big shoes to fill when I took over my dad's firm last year. He was noted as one of the top ten criminal defense attorneys in the nation, and only lost five cases in his thirty-eight-year career before cancer ravaged his body. Winning this case that had gained national attention, feels like a big feather in my hat, confirming that I made the right decision.

DECEPTION

Laura takes me by the hand to a table with a beautiful cake that reads: *Happy 32nd birthday to the best attorney and boss.*

My eyes widen, and my jaw drops open. How could I have forgotten today was my birthday? I was so wrapped up in the case I forgot it was approaching. It's my first birthday without my dad.

My mom pushes through the crowd the moment she sees me frown. I bury my head in her shoulder, while everyone stands in silence, aware of the emotions I'm trying hard to push back.

"It'll be all right, Ames. He's with you every day, and he would never let you go this alone."

Fighting back tears, I pull my head away and offer her a forced smile. "Thank you."

I raise my glass, and mutter, "To a new year filled with more wins and more new shoes."

Everyone claps and downs their champagne.

After lots of cake and more champagne, my colleagues get back to work, and my brother and sister say their goodbyes. My mom hands me a small manila envelope, along with a birthday card. I turn it over and begin to open it, but my mom puts a hand out.

"That one is private, read it when you're by yourself. I want you to know that I'm so proud of you and love you very much." She hugs me tight. "Everything will be all right. Time heals."

As we say goodbye, she reminds me we're due for our girls' weekend. She mentions that she'll speak with Julie, my assistant, to carve out a time on my schedule. Not only can I use such a weekend, but she can too. It's been a long year for her without my dad. He was the rock in her life she so desperately needed.

"Thank you. I don't know how I could have gotten through the last year without you."

"Likewise, Ames. Seeing what a wonderful woman you've become has made it easier for me. I'm so incredibly proud of you and want nothing but happiness for you."

Moments later, I'm back behind my desk, ready to take on a new day filled with criminal law. I stuff the envelope my mom gave to me in my purse so l can read later.

My morning feels like a whirlwind with the attorneys coming in and out of my office, asking for my advice and briefing me on their current cases. A while later, there's a knock on my door. I look up from the computer while Julie strolls in with three gentlemen, all holding breathtakingly large bouquets of roses. This is in true Rich fashion; they have to be from him.

After she advises the delivery guys to put the flowers on the conference table, I go over and remove the card from the envelope with Open First written on the front and read: *Happy Birthday...*

Then, I open the envelope that has the #2 on it and read: *...you thought I forgot...*

A smile forms on my face before I open envelope #3: *...turn around*

Spinning around, I see Rich standing at the door, and a ginormous smile forms on my face. "I asked Julie to keep your afternoon open so that we can do something together." He takes my hand leading me—well, I don't know where to.

He advises me to have a seat in the limo that awaits us at the curb. Handing me a glass, he says, "Let's toast to you being born."

During the car ride, we catch up on the happenings of our day so far. He apologizes for not being at my surprise party, stating he had to leave for work early this morning because clients from England are in town. I shrug. This isn't the first time Rich couldn't make a celebration or event. He owns a prestigious architectural firm, with clients in San Francisco, all round the US, and even in Europe. He lives a busy life, and that is important to him. But he always finds a way to make it up to me, usually in some grand fashion.

As I take my last sip of champagne, the car comes to a stop. "Are you ready?" Rich asks, before exiting the car.

"Ready for what?"

The car door opens, and a hand reaches for mine. When I hear the loud whirling sound, I realize that we're at the airport. "Where are we flying to?"

"Come with me," Rich says, wrapping his arm around my shoulders.

"Your company jet?"

"Step up." He guides me up the stairs of the plane. After leading me to the seat, he bends down announcing we're off to Catalina Island for the afternoon. My heart jumps in excitement. I've been yearning to squish my toes in warm sand.

"Thank you. You really know how to surprise a girl."

"The surprise has only begun," he responds, grinning.

He fetches a bag. Opening it, he reveals a stack of clothes—my clothes—a nicely folded tank top, shorts, and a pair of sandals. "I thought you'd be more comfortable in these," he says, handing them to me.

Standing on tiptoe and putting my arms around his neck, I lean in so our lips meet. He takes me in a quick embrace.

"You better change. We'll be at the island soon."

I pull back and offer a small, playful smile. "Maybe you can help me?"

He winks just as his cell phone rings. After reaching for it in his pocket and looking at who's calling, he tells me he has to take the call. I frown, not feeling so playful anymore, and then scowl at him before going to the restroom.

When I return, he's still on the phone, but announces that he'll call them back later. "What's that?" He points to the envelope that reads: *Ames*, with hand-drawn hearts all over it, which happens to be peaking out of my purse.

"That's from my mom. She gave it to me this morning. She told me to read it when I'm alone. I think she misses my dad."

He narrows his eyes. "I think a lot people still miss him."

Twenty minutes later, the plane lands. After exiting the airport, we're escorted to a limo. "To Avalon," Rich tells the driver. And with a nod of his head, the driver whisks us away.

I grab Rich's hand in mine, resting it on the seat between us. I lay my head on his shoulder and enjoy the beautiful scenery. We reach our destination without a word spoken between us.

The driver opens my door and offers to help me out. The smell from the nearby restaurants and sweet tang of the ocean is invigorating. The island scenery is equally amazing, but one look at Rich exiting the car puts a smile on my face. I have such a beautiful man—one who works hard and provides me with such moments. What more could a girl ask for?

We spend the next two-and-a-half hours eating lunch on the beach and strolling along the boardwalk. I browse in and out of the stores while Rich thumbs through email messages and texts. The time seems so brief when Rich announces we have to return to the airport.

I mope. "We should come back and stay overnight."

"We will someday when we aren't so busy. But I have one more surprise awaiting you, and we can't be late," he tells me, peaking my curiosity.

※

When we're back in San Francisco, Rich directs the limo driver. "Take us to 109 Van Ness Avenue."

Approximately twenty minutes later, we're standing in the parking lot of a car dealership, and I'm staring at a cherry red, 2013 Lamborghini Aventador.

DECEPTION

"Happy birthday."

"Are you serious? This is mine?" Rich nods, raising his eyebrows in confirmation. "Are you sure you can do this? I mean, I don't want you to have to work extra to make this happen."

"Not to worry, Amy. This has been planned for. It's yours. And you don't have to give up your Cadillac either. Get behind the wheel and take me for a spin."

I plant a kiss on his cheek. "Thank you."

After a brief demonstration of the many gadgets from the salesperson, I press down on the gas and we're off. A few moments later, Rich's cell phone chimes. After looking briefly down at it, he tells me I need to drop him off at his firm because the clients from England are waiting for him.

"Is our Friday date night still on?" I ask, already anticipating the answer.

"Sorry, we'll have to take a rain check again this week," he says, not looking away from his phone. I don't respond.

We've taken rain checks far too many times in the last few months. Friday nights were our time, and lately our busy schedules—mostly his—have robbed us of it more times than not.

When we reach his firm, he places a soft kiss on my cheek. "I hope you had a good afternoon. I wish we could have spent more time together. I promise to make it up to you."

"Thank you, Rich," I say warmly.

He exits the car, and I press on the gas pedal, making the tires squeal as I pull away. When I look in my rearview mirror I see Rich smiling and shaking his head.

Once arriving at my law firm, I park the Lamborghini next to my Cadillac convertible. I suppose I'll have to get someone to drive it home for me. Looking around the parking lot, I see a couple of cars remaining. One of them is Julie's, and the other belongs to my best friend, Laura. Just the two people I want to see.

Getting out of the car, something catches my eye. I walk over to the Cadillac and see a sunflower that has been placed on the windshield. I grab it and read the attached tag: *Happy Birthday*

Inside the building, Julie has her nose pressed up against the window while practically drooling. "Is that yours?" she gasps, pointing to my new car.

"Yes. Can you believe it?"

"Wow, Amy, you've got a keeper." I agree, but wish I had more time with him lately. I suppose, that's the price I pay for being with such a successful businessman.

In an attempt to prevent Julie from drowning in the pool of drool, I ask if she's seen anyone around my car.

"No one. Why?" I raise the sunflower so she can see it. "Again?"

"Yeah."

This is the third time a sunflower has shown up on my car window. I found the first one after my dad's funeral. It read: *Thinking of You*. The second one was on Valentine's Day that read: *Spreading a Little Love*. When Rich said it hadn't come from him, I assumed the one on the day of my dad's funeral was from a friend or family member who knew it was the most difficult day of my life. But after receiving the one on Valentine's Day, I called my mom to ask if she knew anything about. My dad had known my favorite flower was a sunflower, and I wondered if he'd arranged to send them to me. She told me she knew nothing about it.

"Whoever it is, I think it's pretty sweet of them," Julie says. "And if it was your dad, as you suspect, it's proof he never wants you to forget him." I smile and tears pool in my eyes. I could never forget him. Ever.

Before the flood gates open, I ask if I have any messages or if there is anything she needs to catch me up on from the day. She hands me a stack of phone messages.

"You got a few calls from clients; one from your mom, who was calling to tell you about the vacation plans she had me put together; and one from Roger, your accountant, asking if you wanted to file an extension for your taxes this year. Oh, and one from Tracy, who claims you've dropped off the face of the earth. She wanted to confirm you were still alive."

"I'll be sure to call her," I respond, wincing. I haven't been able to give much attention to my friends—or family, for that matter—in the last few months since I was so wrapped up in the case. I know they miss me as much as I miss them. "Is Laura still here?"

"I think she's in her office."

"Well, Julie dear, you get home. It's Friday, and I'm sure you have two little ones waiting for you. Have a great weekend. I'll see you Monday. Thank you for waiting for me to get back. You're a true gem."

She smiles and grabs her bag. "I hope you had a great time on the island. Happy birthday, Amy," she responds, heading toward the door.

I peek into Laura's office to find her packing a bag. "I'm glad I caught you before you left."

She looks up. "Hi, Amy. I just finished up the closing arguments for Monday morning."

"Great. I know you have this one wrapped around your finger, but do you need me to do anything?"

"No. I left a copy of the closing arguments on your desk for you to review this weekend."

"Thanks."

Her phone dings, and she looks down. "I have to get going," she says quickly.

"A new guy?" I tease.

"No, I have plans with my sister." She looks nervous—or anxious—for some reason.

"Is everything all right?"

"Yeah. Sorry if I seem distracted. My sister said she needs to talk to me, and that can never be good coming from Sarah."

"Well, don't let me keep you any longer. Call me this weekend if you need anything or want to chat. Otherwise, I'll meet you here at eight o'clock on Monday. We can drive to the courthouse together."

"Okay." On her way to the door, she stops abruptly. "Happy birthday, Amy. We'll have to get together to celebrate sometime next week." She squeezes my hand and then she's gone.

She was really distracted. I won't let it bother me. After all, I've known her my whole life, and she's always panicking about everything and hates being late. I shrug it off and go to my office.

A few seconds later, I hear the muffled sound of my cell phone chiming. "Where in the world did I put it?" I say out loud, trying to locate it. I remember it's in the pocket of my blazer. Taking it out, I notice that there are three missed texts and one voicemail. All the texts are from Tracy.

First text: *Amy Silver, wanted dead or alive.*

I smile.

The second one reads: *Missing: Amy Silver. Hood Milk Company contacted for milk carton advertising.*

I chuckle.

Third text: *Okay, Amy. I'm honestly worried. Where the hell are you? Call me!*

"Oops." I call her.

"I guess I can call off the search dogs now."

"I'm sorry, Tracy. I was stolen away for the afternoon."

"So, I heard. You're lucky your assistant answers her phone."

"I miss your face."

"Come out with me tonight. John and I are meeting up with my old college roommate and her husband for dinner and drinks."

"No way. I refuse to be the fifth wheel."

"Come on, you know with three girls together, the two men will be the fifth wheel. Please come. I miss you, and it's your birthday. Happy birthday, sexy."

I eye the stack of files on my desk. "I really should say yes since my boyfriend has bailed on our Friday date night again, but I have to admit I'm exhausted. It's been a whirlwind of a week, and I have a mountain of case files to review before Monday."

She lets out an exasperated sighs. "I understand, but we haven't been out in forever. Your job has kidnapped you."

I sigh too. "I know. Sorry. I promise that after a few days, I should be back on track. Plus, Laura said she's going to take me out next week for my birthday, so maybe we can make it a group thing."

"Okay." I hear the disappointment in her voice.

"I love you." I blow a kiss into the phone.

"Never as much as I love you. Please call or text me this weekend."

We hang up after agreeing to text over the weekend, and with me promising I won't disappear on her again. I lay my phone on the desk, slump in my chair, and open my email to find thirty-nine unread messages. I really don't want to be doing this on a Friday evening.

After turning the computer off and grabbing the stack of case files and my purse, I lock up behind me on my way out.

At home, I run a bath and fetch a book from the bedroom. I started reading it over two months ago, and I haven't touched it in weeks. Despite wanting to devour every page, I haven't had much time to myself lately. Remembering that I still need to read the letter my mom gave to me this morning, I run downstairs to the entryway, where I left my purse. I reach in, anticipating the letter to be at the top, but I don't feel it. Digging down farther inside, it's not there either.

I turn the light on, hoping I can see it, but it's not there. Flipping my purse over, I dump the contents on the floor. Nothing. I'm puzzled. "What did I do with it?"

I often speak out loud to myself, which happens to be one thing that gets under Rich's skin, so I try not to do it when he's around.

I gather the contents spread out on the floor and put them back in the purse. Trying to think of all of the places I've been to today—almost too many to think of—I realize that I might have dropped it on the plane or maybe in the car. I'm certain I stuffed it down farther into my purse after Rich noticed it peeking out though. Remembering I'm running water for a bath, I rush back to the bathroom. I turn the water off and return to the bedroom to grab the book and my cell phone.

The water feels amazing, and I instantly start to relax. I press three on my cell phone.

"Hi, Ames," my mom answers, but her voice sounds hoarse.

"Are you all right? You don't sound like yourself."

"I think it's a cold."

"Do you want me to come over? I can bring you some soup or medicine."

"No, Ames. I'm fine. Thanks anyway. I have some honey I can take."

After a bit of back and forth, she confesses she knew about my new car and Rich taking me to the island. She tells me that she spoke with Julie to plan our vacation. While detailing our four-day cruise to Baja Mexico next Thursday through Sunday, she adds that the girls' weekend has now turned into a family weekend since she thought it would be nice to invite my brother and sister's family along. I smile in response. We haven't spent a whole lot of time together in a while, so it will be nice. She also called Rich to see if these dates would work for him, but he told her he's unsure at the moment. He thinks he may have to go to England sometime in the next couple of weeks. This is the first I hear about it.

"I'll talk to him. We'll work it out," I console her.

After a bit more chatter, we get ready to say goodbye. "Did you read your letter yet?"

I hesitate to tell her I can't find it. I don't want to sound like I was careless. But before I can even think of how to respond, I blurt, "I haven't yet. I think I dropped it on Rich's plane this afternoon. I plan to get it first thing in the morning."

She's silent for a minute. "Oh, all right."

Why didn't I tell her I hadn't read it yet? Why couldn't my mouth wait for my brain to function before opening up and speaking? I try to think on my feet. "I love you. I hope you feel better," I say, attempting to divert her attention.

"I love you too, Ames. Call me this weekend."

After hanging up, I lay my head back and start to read.

I'm woken by the sound of the front door closing downstairs. Glancing at the clock on the wall, I see it's eleven-thirty-five. I hit the drain with my foot and get out of the tub. After wrapping my robe around me, I head downstairs to find Rich rummaging through the fridge.

"Did I wake you?" he asks without turning around.

"Yes, but I'm glad you did." He pops a few blueberries into his mouth. "Would you like me to make you something to eat? I can cook you an omelet."

He shakes his head. "I want to take a shower and get to bed. It's been a long day," he murmurs.

"Yeah, you're home late."

"It's a long story. The guys from England are proposing something I'm not sure I want to be a part of."

"That's too bad. You seem to have established a good relationship with them over the past couple of years."

"I know. And that's part of the problem," he says, pressing his lips together, looking annoyed. "Let's get to bed."

I lace my arm into his. We turn off the lights while making our way upstairs. "You know it is still Friday," I say, looking up at him suggestively.

He grins. "Give me a few minutes to shower, and I'll be right there."

I lie in bed listening to the sound of the water, and it practically lulls me to sleep. Rich finally comes into the bedroom and lies down next to me.

"I'm exhausted, babe. Do you think we could take a rain check until tomorrow?" he asks, turning off the bedside light.

"Of course," I respond with too little energy to argue.

Wrapping an arm around him, I push up against his back and lightly kiss his shoulder. He takes my hand in his, and we drift off to sleep.

chapter two

Saturday
April 13, 2013
7:18 a.m.

Rolling over, I notice Rich's side of the bed is empty.

Stretching my arms over my head, I contemplate sleeping for a bit longer, but suddenly my bladder starts screaming. I push back the covers and sit on the edge of the bed, while rubbing the sleep out of my eyes.

When I exit the bathroom I can smell coffee, and immediately start to feel awake. I saunter downstairs toward the kitchen, wondering if Rich had left any coffee for me. When I reach the bottom of the stairs, I hear muffled voices coming from the home office.

As I draw closer, I notice that the door is closed. He never closes the door unless he's in a meeting or on a teleconference. I look out the living room window to see if there's anyone here besides Rich, but only my new car and his SUV are in the driveway.

I tiptoe over to the door and put my ear up to it, hoping to make out some words.

"I'm not going to do it," Rich says in a much angrier tone than I've ever heard him use. "I don't care. You're not going to do this to me and my business." Then I hear the sound of the telephone being slammed down. It makes my insides jump. My feet are glued in place, and I'm unsure of what to do next. If I stay in this spot, he'll open the door and see I've been eavesdropping.

My brain finally wakes my feet up from under me, and I start toward the kitchen just when Rich opens the door. "Good morning," he says, and it sounds more like a question than a statement.

I smile. "Good morning," I respond, trying not to let him see my concern for what I overheard. "Did you make some coffee?"

"Yes, and I left you a cup. I have to head out in a few. The guys from England are leaving today, and I have to meet with them before they go," he says from behind me.

"Is everything all right?"

There's a pause. "It will be," he says, huffing.

I turn around when I remember that I, too, have something to do this morning. "Can I get William's phone number?"

Rich furrows his brow and tilts his head to the side. "William, my pilot? Why do you need his number?"

"I think I may have dropped the letter my mom gave me yesterday on the plane. I thought it was in my purse, but I can't find it."

"That's… too bad," he says after a long pause. "I can call William on my way into work to see if he found it."

"That would be perfect. Thank you."

Twenty minutes later, he kisses me on the forehead and rushes out the door after I remind him to call me as soon as he speaks to William.

Three hours pass, and I have yet to hear from Rich. Growing anxious, I text him: *Hate to bother you, but have you called William yet?*

I put my phone down and continue looking over the case files, sitting in the lounge chair by the pool. My stomach growls and I realize I haven't eaten breakfast yet. I gather the stack of files and go inside to make some eggs and bacon.

While eating, I run over everything I need to do this weekend. Remembering that I never returned my accountant's call from yesterday, I dial Roger's number.

"Amy, good to hear from you," he answers, after just one ring.

"Hi, Roger. Sorry I never called you back."

"Not to worry. How is everything?"

"Good, I guess. Does it look like I'll be able to keep the firm alive for another year?" I joke.

"I'd like to hope so. I don't plan to retire for another ten years," he shoots back, and I hear the smile in his voice.

"Do you think we should file for an extension?"

"I do, Amy. With the change in ownership within the past year, I think we need a bit more time to get everything together."

"That works for me. Let me know what you need from me, all right?"

"I will. Congratulations on the big win. I know that was probably your biggest case. You sure are making your dad proud."

"Thanks, Roger. That means a lot coming from you."

"Are you home or at your office? I need to fax over some paperwork for you to sign, and I need to do so today since the deadline for the extension is tomorrow."

"You can fax it to my home office number."

"I'll do that right now. You just need to sign the first page and fax it back to me."

"Thank you. I couldn't manage without you."

"You're welcome. Take care of yourself. Talk to you soon."

I hang up, thinking how great a relationship my dad and Roger had. He was my dad's accountant from the first day he opened up the firm. My dad had many long-term relationships, friendships, and connections which really benefited his career. I could only hope for the same.

I check my phone to see if Rich texted back, but he hasn't. He must be in a meeting. I hope it's going well. This morning's phone call didn't sound so great. The stress of his successful—but demanding—business has put a damper on our relationship. Not that he meant for it to, it just does. We don't get to spend time together as we once did, and when we do, it's always disrupted by phone calls, texts, and emails. I get that he doesn't work a Monday through Friday, nine to five job, but I don't think he anticipated his business would ever become this demanding.

Hearing the fax machine, I go to the office and grab the papers as they come through. Looking around for a pen, I don't find one. I rummage through the drawers of my desk unsuccessfully. "Why do I lose everything lately?"

Searching Rich's desk, I still come up empty-handed. I open a drawer and feel inside, hoping to find a pen—or even a pencil at this point—but find neither. Opening another drawer, I pull too hard, and all of its contents fall to the floor. Defeated, I plop myself down, thinking Rich will be upset that I created a mess of his impeccable organization. All off a sudden, something catches my eye. It's a cell phone. Similar to one I had in college—it's a simple flip phone, not nearly as fancy as the iPhone. Flipping it open, I see TracFone written below the screen. Isn't a TracFone a prepaid cell phone?

My curiosity is peaked so I press a button. It must have some charge left because it powers up and the home screen appears. Unsure of what I'm looking for, I push a series of buttons, and one pulls up a screen of text messages. Clicking the first one in the list, I immediately freeze. My whole body goes numb for a second, and then fires back up. I scroll through the long list of messages.

Outgoing Message: *Meet you at the restaurant at 7 tonight.*

Incoming Message: *Where have you been? Call me, I miss you.*

Incoming Message: *You're the sexiest man I've ever laid eyes on.*

Outgoing Message: *I can't wait to kiss every inch of your body.*

I rub my hand across my face and shake my head. This can't be happening. My stomach hurts, and I can't get myself to scroll to another message. These texts have to be from before we were together. That would make the most sense. I look for dates and find, February 14, 2012. My heart drops, and a lump forms in my throat. That is not an old message. That's about three months before my dad passed away. This cannot be Rich's phone. It can't be. I run through countless reasons why he would have it. Maybe one of his friends gave it to him to hold onto for some odd reason? Nervous, I feel guilty for rummaging through his belongings.

I put the contents from his desk back into the drawer, but hold on to the phone, unwilling to let go of it. After quickly placing it in my pocket, I slide the drawer back into the desk. Worried Rich will walk in and see me sitting on the floor by his desk, I jump to my feet and go to the door. Remembering that I never signed the papers Roger needs, I turn around. As I do, I notice a pen lying right by the fax machine. I sign the first page and fax it back.

I run upstairs and shut the door to the bedroom behind me. In a panic, I go over to the closet and hide the phone under clothes stacked on the top shelf. Deciding that I need to get out of the house, I grab my cell phone and keys, and rush out the front door.

I don't know where I'm headed, but I've been driving south on the highway for over an hour when my phone chimes. Pulling off at the next exit, I find the nearest gas station.

I take out my phone and read a text from Rich: *Talked to William. He checked the plane and your letter isn't there. I should be home in a couple of hours.*

I rest my head against the headrest. Should I come out and ask him about it? Should I try to find out more information before confronting him in case I'm jumping to conclusions?

DECEPTION

I dial Laura's number, but it only rings until her voicemail picks up.

Looking around, I realize that I'm not even sure how I got here. It appears to be a small town, and close by is a beach and the ocean. There's a bar and grill off the beach, aside from a few shops. Thinking that they might have outside seating where I could have a drink and gather my thoughts, I cross the street and park.

Glancing at the front door to see if the place is open since it looks dark inside, I read the hours posted: *11:00 am to 1:00 am Monday thru Sunday.*

I walk in and I'm greeted by the hostess. "Welcome to the Love Shack. I'm Izzy. Would you like a table or a seat at the bar?" I ask to sit outside. "Of course, ma'am, all of our tables are outdoors," she responds in a high-pitched, overly cheerful tone. Did she call me ma'am? I understand she's young—maybe pushing seventeen—but do I really look old enough to be called ma'am? She walks me through the bar area where the bartender chats with customers. He briefly looks my way and nods.

"Is this table good for you, ma'am?"

"Yes, this is perfect. Thank you."

"Ana will be right over to take your order," she says, placing the menu on the table in front of me.

This place is beautiful. It sits right off of the beach, overlooking the ocean. And in the distance there's a lighthouse. I'm surprised to see not many people on the beach—there are only maybe ten or so, and they aren't even dressed in bathing suits. Nearby there are rows of white wooden chairs facing the ocean, and an archway is draped in red silk fabric. It must be for a wedding. If there was a perfect place to get married, this would be it.

I'm interrupted. "Hi, I'm Ana, and I'll be your waitress for today. Welcome to the Love Shack. Can I get you a drink while you look at the menu?" She has the same high-pitched, overly cheerful tone that the hostess did. Wondering if that's a requirement to work here, I inwardly giggle to myself.

"Yes, please. May I have a red raspberry martini with Chambord?"

"Of course."

When she returns with my drink, she takes my order. Once she's gone, I grab my cell phone out of my bag and dial Tracy's number. I really need a friend right now, someone who can talk some sense into me. The line rings, and when her voicemail picks up I leave her a message: "I was really hoping you would answer, please call me."

DECEPTION

Not more than ten minutes later, the waitress returns with my food. "This place is beautiful," I remark.

"Yes, ma'am. It is." Did she call me ma'am as well? What a crappy day this has turned out to be. "I've been working here for a year now and really love it. Many of my friends work here too. Everyone is really nice. We often host events and parties. We're hosting that wedding this evening. There's going to be over two hundred guests so it should be a good night for tips."

"That's great," I say, thinking that she gave me more information than I bargained for.

Taking a bite out of my salad, that's her cue to walk away. "Let me know if you need anything," she says, before turning and heading back inside.

After finishing my salad and drink, I pay the tab and head back through the bar. This is exactly the kind of place I needed to help clear my head. Izzy opens the door for me.

"Thank you for visiting the Love Shack. We hope you plan to return soon. Have a nice day, ma'am," she says, making my skin crawl.

I rush out and head back to my car, thinking that I have to make an appointment to see my stylist soon. My gray hairs must be showing.

Once I'm back in San Francisco, I have no desire to go home so I decide to do some shopping instead. Shopping is always my best friend when my real friends are busy—actually, anytime is a good time for retail therapy. And while out, hopefully Tracy or Laura will call me back. I don't want to be home with Rich when they do. As I exit the car, my phone dings. It's an incoming text message from Rich: *I just got home, where are you?*

Not really wanting to give anything away, but also not interested in talking to him right now, I keep my response brief: *Out shopping.*

He writes back: *I stopped by your firm to pick up your Cadillac. I had Dennis drive it home for you.*

Me: *Thanks.*

After strolling through the stores, and spending way more money than I should have, I load the bags into the car when my phone rings. After fumbling for it in my bag, I look at who's calling. Seeing it's Tracy, I immediately answer it, feeling relieved.

"What's wrong?" She sounds panicked.

DECEPTION

I exhale. "Tracy, I found something while rummaging through Rich's desk this morning. And I'm not sure what I should do about it."

"Do you want to come over? I'm home alone. Where are you?"

"Are you busy? I don't want to put a damper on your—"

"Get over here," she utters out before I can finish.

Fifteen minutes later, we're sitting in her backyard holding a martini. "Tell me all about it girl. Tell me everything."

I tell her why I was rummaging through his desk and what I found. "It had well over thirty text messages, but I couldn't get myself to look at them all. Part of me was in shock, another part was feeling guilty for going through his personal stuff, and another part was downright sick. All of the texts were to and from someone named Olivia."

"And you're sure that these messages aren't from before you two got together?"

"The latest message was from Valentines of last year." While trying to recall what we did on Valentine's Day, I'm reminded that I spent it alone because Rich was in Chicago on business—or so that's what he told me.

"Am I the only one that you've told?"

"Yes. I called Laura but she didn't answer her phone. I've been going crazy, needing to talk to someone all day."

"Well, let's try to think this through and figure out what you should do. If you confront him now with little information to go on besides what you read, you may end up wrong and then lose his trust. But if you don't confront him now, you may never be able to trust him ever again because you'll always wonder. But... if you go with plan C, you could always do a bit more digging before you say or do anything. And I could even help."

"Where do I even start?" I ask, feeling defeated.

"Check his current cell phone for an 'Olivia' listed in his contacts. Look for any text messages that may be suspicious. Rummage through his desk some more and review the rest of the text messages on the phone you found. That's where I'd start. Hopefully in the process, you find out that it's not even his cell phone."

"I should get home before he starts to wonder what's up."

"Don't start feeling guilty for what you found. It'll show on your face and then, yes, he will start wondering what is up. You have every right to find out if that phone is his, and if it is, why he felt the need to be with someone else."

Getting up, I hug her. She kisses my cheek. "Call me, no matter what time it is."

"Thank you for always being there for me."

Standing in front of my dad's grave, I'm not sure why I ended up driving here instead of going home. After sitting down, I brush off the grass and weeds from around the stone. "I wish you were here with me right now. I'm not sure what's happening to my life, but it feels like it's crashing down around me. I'm afraid of what the next few days and weeks ahead are going to reveal. I don't think I can take having my heart shattered one more time. I don't think I can get through it. I miss you so much. You were my rock, daddy. You were the one there to pick me up and hold me up every time life got hard." I sob so hard that my whole body trembles.

After watching the sun go down, I find my composure and plant a kiss on the headstone. Walking to the car, I feel stronger. But I still know that I have to figure out what comes next.

When I get home, Rich is in the office typing on the computer. My stomach begins to ache. "You can do this," I advise myself.

Taking a deep breath, I stand in the doorway. "Hi."

Rich raises his head in my direction. "Hi. I'm glad you're home. Did you have a good time shopping?" he asks, looking down at the bags in my hands.

"Yes, it was nice. Did you eat?"

"No, I was waiting for you. You took a while. I was getting ready to put some burgers on the grill and make a salad."

"Burgers and salad sound good."

After turning off the computer, he gets up from the chair. He walks in my direction, and then pauses. "Are you all right? You look like you've been crying."

"I stopped at my dad's grave."

He nods in acknowledgement and plants a kiss on my cheek. "He's watching over you."

"Yeah. I know. Let me put my bags away and I'll help you prepare dinner," I respond, turning to make my way upstairs.

"I think we have a couple of steaks we can throw on too," he adds, walking in the kitchen.

We decide to take our dinner to the living room and watch a movie. While flipping through the movie selections, he clears his throat. "So, your mom planned a cruise for next week?"

"Yeah, she said that she spoke to you about it. Will you be able to take time off?"

"I think so. I have to move a few things around, but I should be able to make it happen."

Surprised by his response, I offer a smile. "Great. It'll be nice to have my family together. We haven't done much since my dad died." He nods, not taking his eyes off the television.

We settle on watching The Hangover. We've both seen the movie quite a few times, but it never gets old. He sits at one end of the couch, and lying down at the other end, I rest my feet on his legs. Throughout the movie I can't help but think about the TracFone and what he could possibly be hiding from me. I keep glancing over at him and he looks as distracted as I am. A few times our eyes meet and we grin or quickly look away. I'm trying not to look like something is up, but it's hard.

Once the movie ends, Rich leans over and rubs my arm. "Can I take you to the bedroom?" he asks, grinning. Quite surprised by his words—it's not Friday after all—I grab his hand and we stroll upstairs.

After taking our clothes off, Rich turns off the bedside light and I get in bed. He lies down next to me and kisses my neck. Then he reaches my mouth, occupying it, while I try to get the text messages out of my mind. He brushes the hair away from my ear. "Are you okay?" he asks, noticing that I'm pre-occupied in thought.

"Yes, of course," I say, breathy, and then pull him in for a kiss. All the while, I try to remain focused on what we're doing—what I'm supposed to be doing.

chapter three

Sunday
April 14, 2013
1:07 a.m.

Unable to fall asleep, I lie in bed listening to the sound of Rich snoring. I venture downstairs and head to the kitchen for a glass of water. Passing by the office, I notice that he left the light on. Reaching in to flip the switch, I see his iPhone sitting on his desk. I contemplate if it's a good time to search through his contacts and messages.

Hearing him snore upstairs, I rush to his desk and grab the phone. Rushing back out, I hurry down the hallway to the bathroom. After shutting the door behind me, I slide myself down to the floor and press the power button. Anticipating the home screen to appear, my finger freezes in place and I stare down in disbelief. The screen asks for a combination. He put a lock on his phone? No, no, no. He can't have his phone locked. Why does he have his phone locked?

I press a variety of number combinations, hoping that one of them will unlock the phone. But none of them do. Laying the phone down on the floor, I stare at the wall. How am I supposed to find out anything now? "Damn it," I say a bit too loud.

Getting up from the floor, I bend down and grab the phone. After slowly opening the bathroom door, I look out cautiously. All I hear is the sound of Rich snoring upstairs. I tip-toe back to the office and put the phone on his desk in the exact position that it was found.

After turning the light off, I meander to the kitchen and grab a bottle of water from the refrigerator. I stand at the patio door, looking up at the night sky. Despite wanting to look at the rest of the text messages on the TracFone, I convince myself that it's too risky since it's upstairs in my bedroom closet. I decide to go back to bed and wait until tomorrow instead.

DECEPTION

Waking up to the sound of the front door closing, I turn and look at the clock on my nightstand, it's five o'clock. Interested to see where he could be headed off to on a Sunday morning this early, I get up and stumble downstairs. Looking out the window, I see his SUV in the driveway, which means that he went for a run.

I head back upstairs and snuggle back into bed. I pull the covers up to my ear, close my eyes, but sleep doesn't come. My mind starts racing again. Turning over on my back, I think about grabbing the TracFone. His runs normally take at least an hour—a whole hour to figure things out.

I get out of bed and walk to the closet, reaching up on the shelf for the phone. Taking it in my hand, I decide to stand by the bedroom door to hear the front door open when he returns. I flip the phone open and the main screen shows. Glancing at the battery icon on the top right, I see it's showing one red bar—there's not much power left. After pressing a button, the contact list shows. Only one number is listed and I try to make a mental note of what it is.

I press another button and the text message list pops up again. Scanning the list, I reach the ones that I didn't read yesterday.

Outgoing Message (February 14, 2012, 1:05pm): *I'll show you just how lucky you are tonight {{wink}}*

Incoming Message (February 14, 2012, 12:54pm): *How could I be so lucky to have you? xoxo*

Outgoing Message (February 14, 2012, 12:51pm): *I was able to get out of my meeting early, so I'm leaving Chicago now. I'll call you when we land. I made plans for dinner at 6 at our favorite restaurant.*

Incoming Message (February 14, 2012, 12:32pm): *Haven't heard from you. Please tell me you're coming over tonight.*

Outgoing Message (February 14, 2012, 9:36am): *I'm trying*

Incoming Message (February 14, 2012, 9:04am): *Can we christen my new sofa tonight? I have a special Valentines outfit waiting for you.*

Incoming Message (February 13, 2012, 3:24am): *I can now go to sleep. Thank you for calling me so that I can hear the sound of your voice. That sexy voice!*

Incoming Message (February 13, 2012, 1:58am): *I'm awake. Can you call me?*

Outgoing Message (February 13, 2012, 1:56am): *Awake and thinking of you.*

DECEPTION

Outgoing Message (February 12, 2012, 2:48pm): *Thank you for the incredible lunch date... and dessert.*

Feeling like I'm going to be sick, I run to the bathroom and hurl into the toilet. My pulse quickens and my face becomes hot. Anger rages and I throw the phone before I can even think. It goes flying out of the bathroom and across the bedroom. It smashes against the dresser and lands on the floor in pieces. As soon as I realize what I've done, I run to it, dropping to the floor. While I gather the pieces, I realize that I don't have the battery. While reaching under the dresser, I hear the front door open downstairs. "Shit." I push myself up and run to the closet. Reaching up, I put the pieces of the phone back under the stack of clothes on the shelf.

Rushing back to the bathroom, I shut the door behind me. Staring into the mirror, I try to decide what to do next. I'm not ready to confront him yet, and I need to talk to Tracy again. Taking in a deep breath, I open the door and go lie back in bed, pulling the covers over my head.

Minutes later, Rich walks upstairs and into the bedroom. I don't move. He puts his clothes into the hamper and walks to the bathroom, shutting the door behind him. He turns on the shower, and the sound of the water lulls me back to sleep.

I'm awakened by Rich hovering over me. "I have to go out for a few. Your mom sent a text saying that she won't be making it to church today."

Barely awake, I nod. He walks away and I glance at the clock, it's seven-eleven. I need to get up and ready for the nine o'clock church service. My mom and I have been meeting up for Sunday morning service every week since my dad passed.

I get out of bed and head downstairs to grab my phone to call her. Walking over to the table in the entryway, I notice my phone isn't there. But I remember leaving it there last night. Once I make my way to the kitchen, I see it lying on the counter next to the coffee maker. While certain that I didn't leave it there, I try and shake it off. The phone reads that I have one unread text message.

My mom: *Good morning Ames. I won't be making it to mass this morning. I'm still not feeling well. Please don't worry, I just want to rest. Call me later today. Love you.*

How did Rich know that she texted me? Was he looking through my phone? Did he read the text as it came through? Putting my phone down, I contemplate going to church alone but decide to pass today. Today's the day to gather myself and do a bit of confronting.

DECEPTION

While exiting the shower, I hear my phone ringing downstairs. After drying off and getting dressed, I head down to see who called. I have one new voicemail, it's from Tracy. She asks if I want to spend the day with her and a few friends, so I call her back.

"Amy."

"Hey, Tracy. I'm surprised you're awake so early on a Sunday morning," I quip.

"Hey now, go easy on me. Fine. Alison texted at eight o'clock to see if we could do something today. I wasn't exactly awake when she did. But I am now," she jokes in return. "So, do you want to join us? We want to go to the beach. Alison is calling Laura to see if she wants to come too."

"Sure, I guess I'll go."

"Is everything all right? Did you find anything else out from yesterday?"

"I did look at his iPhone, but he has a lock on it."

"No fucking way, Amy. He's setting himself up for being guilty."

"I know. But, in his defense, he could have it locked because it's also his work phone. He may have a lot of important contacts and information in it. You know, if he should happen to lose it, it would be awful."

"That excuse sounds good and all, but do you really want to believe that?"

"I don't know what to believe," I say, overwhelmed by the whole situation. "I read more of the text messages on the TracFone. It made me vomit, literally."

"That's it. You need to get dressed because we're going to the beach today. We're going to figure out what you do from here. You have to fill me in on what the texts said. Actually, take the phone with you. We can snoop through it for you. It'll save you the heartache of having to see anything more."

"I'm not sure the phone works anymore," I say, cringing. "I kind of smashed it up against the dresser."

She lets out a small giggle. "Oops. Well, then we'll have to come up with a Plan B."

"Yup."

Forty minutes later, Tracy is ringing the doorbell. I greet her at the door and she stands there looking at me without saying a word. "What's the matter?"

"What is that parked in your driveway?" she asks, pointing to my new car.

I smirk. "Rich bought it for my birthday."

"Well, I guess there has to be more to the text messages because there's no way that a cheating boyfriend would buy his girlfriend a car that costs over three-hundred-thousand dollars." She gasps. "Holy shit, Amy."

"I know," I say, having thought the same thing.

"We're taking your car today," she says, smiling wide. "Alison and Laura can take their own car."

When Laura and Alison arrive, I'm in the middle of showing Tracy the inside of the car. "Damn girl," Alison remarks, getting out of her Jeep.

"Hi," I say, feeling embarrassed. I've never been the flashy type, or to put myself on display for having money. And this car does the exact opposite of that.

"Is this your car?" Laura asks.

"Can you believe it? Rich got this for her birthday," Tracy says, in shock.

"Wow."

"So which beach are we headed to today?" I ask, trying to change the subject.

"Not sure, we haven't gotten that far in our planning yet," Tracy says.

"I know of a little beach about an hour from here. Do you want to do that?" They all nod in agreement, not taking their eyes off of the car.

An hour or so later, we're parked down from the Love Shack and they're remarking how nice this little town is. We take our beach towels, umbrellas, and bags, and head down to the beach. It's evident that it is going to be packed today. People are already laid out and in the water. We find a spot to spread out our towels and umbrellas a bit to the left of the Love Shack.

Laura has me tell the girls what I discovered yesterday. Alison convinces herself that he's guilty, and Tracy seems to be in agreement. But Laura remains quiet, looking disgusted, when I summarize what was read on the phone. Laura's known me since we were kids. She's been through a lot with me, and she's helped me get through a lot. I think she doesn't want this to happen to me, especially at this point in my life.

My phone chimes, so I search for it in my bag. It's Rich: *Stuck at work, I will be home later than I anticipated. I'll call you on my way home.*

I read the text out loud and Alison shoots me a muddled look.

I text back: *Okay. I'm at the beach with the girls. Won't be home until late.*

After turning my phone off, I shove it down to the bottom of my bag. "I'm done talking about it. I want a day to relax and take in the sun," I say to the girls, wanting nothing more than to push everything out of thought.

"Please promise us that you won't confront him until you do a bit more digging, all right?" Tracy asks, shooting me a knowing glance. I nod, but I'm not sure that I'll be able to do that.

We spend the rest of the morning taking in the sun and reading, while chatting about celebrities, fashion, and life.

"So, Laura, is everything okay with your sister?" I ask, remembering our Friday exchange.

She puts down her magazine and groans. "She's pregnant," she announces, disappointed.

"Oh goodness."

Laura's twenty-seven-year-old sister, Sarah, hasn't necessarily had an easy and successful life. She's been through countless jobs since barely graduating from college. Laura even managed to convince Rich to hire her as a receptionist at his firm, but that lasted only six months. He had to let her go because she was calling out so much. She still lives with her parents and has been temping at various places since. She can't seem to get her life together.

"Yeah," Laura says, pressing her lips together and shaking her head. "She's in a bad situation." We all offer looks of concern.

In the near distance, music begins to play; a disc jockey is set up on the patio of the Love Shack. We look at each other, wide-eyed, in excitement.

"This place rocks," Alison exclaims, bouncing to the beat of the music.

"I told you guys that I found a gem," I say, enthusiastic.

Needing to find a restroom, we decide to have lunch on the patio of the Love Shack. We're greeted by Izzy, or maybe it's Ana, I don't recall who's who. She recognizes me the moment she greets us. "Nice to see you, ma'am. We're happy you decided to visit the Love Shack again," she says in her most annoyingly, high-pitched voice. The girls smile in response. I snarl at them. Izzy—or Ana—doesn't even pick up on it. She escorts us to our table, letting us know that Marcus will be over to take our order.

"Did she call you ma'am?" Tracy asks, laughing, when Izzy—or Ana—walks away.

"Shut up," I say flippantly.

We spend the rest of the afternoon sipping drinks, enjoying music, swapping stories, and laughing. It looks like the sun is about to set so I look at the clock, it's five-forty-five. I'm shocked that we spent the entire day here and it feels like we've just arrived. Deciding that we should head back home, Laura go to the restroom before we leave.

She comes back, gushing. "They have the sweetest thing. There's a 'Soul Mates' wall by the bathrooms. It's

DECEPTION

plastered with photos of couples," she says, melting into the floor.

I scrunch up my face. "Puke."

They laugh, knowing how much I don't believe in soul mates—and certainly not now, more than ever.

"Do you think he's there?" Tracy asks.

"I don't know, but I want to drive by to see."

On my way home, I decide to pass by Rich's firm to see if his car is there, not really anticipating him to be at this time. Pulling into the parking lot behind the building, I sigh with relief. The lot is empty.

"Well, he's not here. He must be at home." The moment I say the last word, my relief turns into panic. I don't think I can be in the same house with him right now, having read those texts this morning. I'm not confident that I can hold myself together and not confront him.

"Don't say anything, Amy," Tracy warns, knowing exactly what I'm thinking. "We will figure this out. You need more to go on than a smashed up TracFone at this point." I gaze at her with a look of defeat.

We arrive at my house, and much to my surprise there are only two cars in the driveway. Neither of them is Rich's SUV—only my Cadillac and Tracy's BMW. "Where the hell is he?" Tracy questions, mirroring my shock.

"I have no idea."

We sit there staring at each other. "Do you want to drive around and see if we can spot him?"

"I don't even know where to look. San Fran is quite big."

"Dammit, Amy. It is past seven o'clock on a Sunday night. Where the heck could he be at this time?"

"He might be with Daniel or another of his friends," I say, shrugging. Shaking her head, she doesn't say anything, but also doesn't look convinced. "I'm not calling him. I'm not interested in listening to any of his lies. I really need to get inside and shower, and then get focused for court in the morning."

"Text or call me when he gets home."

"All right."

Walking in the house, I note that it looks exactly as I left it this morning. I don't think he's been home all day. I bustle upstairs, and plop down on the bed, feeling exhausted.

Feeling a chill, I turn over to my side and notice that I'm lying on top of the covers. Glancing over at the clock, I realize that I fell asleep—in my beach clothes—and have been sleeping for well over three hours. Noticing that Rich's side of the bed is empty, I get up. Approaching the bedroom door, I can hear the television downstairs and see the lights on. I grab my pajamas from my dresser and head into the bathroom. After turning on the shower, I get in.

When I come back out of the bathroom, the television is still on downstairs. Too tired to be interested in seeing what he's doing, I decide to head straight back to bed.

When I awake, Rich isn't in bed. I get up and stroll downstairs for a cup of coffee. I notice that his SUV is not in the driveway so he must've already left for the day.

While drinking my coffee, I review Laura's closing arguments. Feeling confident that it'll be an easy morning in court, I get dressed, pack my bag, and grab my cell phone. I drive off to meet up with Laura at the firm, deciding to use my Cadillac today.

chapter four

Monday
April 15, 2013
10:11 a.m.

Forcefully pushing through the courtroom doors, I storm into the hallway. Making my way through the sea of reporters, I shield my face with my arm while waves of cameras flash. I bolt to the doors of the courthouse and rush outside, not looking anywhere but in the direction of the car that is waiting for us at the bottom of the stairs.

The driver opens the door for me, but before he can close it, I grab hold of it and slam it shut, hard. Laura must have been right behind me because she slides into the seat on the other side.

With both fists, I punch the seat in front of me. "What the hell happened in there? This can't be fucking happening right now. My career is ruined. I'm now the laughingstock of San Fran. Shit! Dammit! I lost my first case, and all because of a sadistic monster." Laura sits in silence. Feeling sick, I bend forward, wrapping my arms around my waist.

"I'm sorry, Amy. I had no idea that he was insane. He never once let up that he could be the monster behind it all. This wasn't your loss. I was lead council on this case, and it's my fault this happened. It's my loss," she says, in a barely audible tone. I swallow hard, trying to find my equanimity. My head spins and my insides shake.

The driver starts the car and drives off while reporters pound on the windows and stand in our path, yelling out questions. "How does it feel to defend Satan?" one reporter shouts in the massive sea of words.

I peep at Laura who's sitting still, with her head resting back. "How could this have happened? I reviewed this case from top to bottom, countless times. I met with him, like you did. There is no way we could have predicted he would have said what he did in there.

It's not your fault. I also thought we had this one in the bag. This was a simple, open and shut case in my book. No one saw this coming."

"Dammit," she mutters through clenched teeth.

The Prosecution was presenting their closing arguments to the jury when our client, Gordon, jumps up from his seat. "I'm guilty! I killed that bitch, and I'd do it again too," he proclaims, vividly. Gasps are heard from the entire courtroom. Four police officers rush to him. "God came to me last night. He told me that if I don't confess, I'll be nailed to the cross and sent to the depths of hell for eternity. That bitch deserved to be cleansed. She was impure, she was vile, and she was rotting from the inside. I did it. I killed her before she could infect anyone else," he shouts, amidst all the disorder. He puts his hands together like he's praying and looks up at the ceiling. "I did it, Lord. I did what I needed to do. I did it for you." The police escort him out of the courtroom. Every single person in the room sits in silence. We are all in disbelief—in complete, and utter, shock.

The person that Gordon confessed to killing—to cleansing— was his sister. She was a well-known hooker and drug addict. He convinced us that he was trying to help her get clean and off the streets. She was found in a rundown motel with her feet and hands strapped to the bed, and it looked like she had choked on her own vomit. Fingerprints retrieved at the scene came back with a match for Gordon, which is when he was taken into custody and hired us. He claimed that she called him that evening because she said she was afraid. She felt someone was following her. We even spoke with family members who backed his story, saying that Gordon was always the one Beth would call when she was in need or in trouble. He seemed like a sane, and caring, brother.

"We should've taken the insanity plea when they offered it to us."

"I suppose, in hindsight."

"It's possible for some people to snap."

Apparently the news spread like wildfire, because everyone at the firm appears to know what happened. Everyone scatters to their desks and offices when we arrive, except for my assistant, Julie, who comes running to me.

"I'm sorry, Amy," she says, hugging me.

Laura makes a bee-line to her office, and I to mine. Slumping down in my chair, I stare out the window into the city. "Sorry I let you down, Dad. I gave your life's work a bad name. I'm not as smart as you thought I was."

"Amy?" Julie utters, standing at the door. I twist my chair to face her. "I hate to bother you, but I wanted to tell you that Mrs. Collins called to reschedule her three o'clock appointment."

"All right."

"Rich also called here twice. He said you aren't answering your phone or responding to your text messages. I told him you were in court this morning. He asked me to have you call him when you got back."

I roll my eyes. "Thank you, Julie."

Rich is the last person I want to think about right now, and that saddens me. He's the one person I should be able to lean on the most, but he doesn't seem very trustworthy at the moment. I'm feeling alone, regardless of the amount of friends, colleagues, and family I have.

Busying myself the rest of the afternoon, no one dares to come to me all day, not even Laura. At the end of the day, Julie saunters in, handing me my schedule for tomorrow. "I had to move a few meetings around. We got a call from a gentleman regarding the possible homicide out in Half Moon on Friday."

"What homicide is that?"

"You didn't hear about it? It's the one where a husband and wife were stabbed to death in their home. It was on the news all weekend."

"No. I didn't have the television on this weekend. Who wants to meet with me?"

"It's one of the couple's sons. He said that his brother was taken into custody, and now he's being questioned as well. He was adamant about speaking to you. I offered for him to speak with Doug, since his schedule is open tomorrow, but he said he wanted to speak with you directly. I moved your one o'clock meeting with the Littletons to next Monday, after you get back from your cruise. I hope that's okay."

"That's fine. I'm certain no one will want to speak with me after today's court frenzy is all over the news anyway."

"Don't be so hard on yourself. Sometimes people are so good at lying, that they begin to believe their own story. That had to be why he was so convincing. You're a top-notch lawyer, Amy. Don't fool yourself into believing otherwise."

"Thank you, Julie."

I sit dumbfounded for the next couple of hours, while watching the attorneys and employees leave for the day. Not having seen Laura since this morning, I go to her office but find it empty.

Returning, I decide that I better call Rich before he sends out the search dogs. Realizing that the phone battery is dead, I plug it into the wall to let it power up.

Three voicemails await me. Not feeling much like listening to them, I press one and wait for Rich answer. His voicemail picks up, which sends a wave of relief through me.

I leave a message: "Hey Rich, sorry I haven't called you today. Court was crazy this morning, as I'm sure you've already heard. And my phone was dead. I should be home soon."

Resting my elbows on the desk, I cradle the heavy weight of my head in my hands, feeling defeated, exhausted, and angry about today… and my life.

Arriving home, I round the corner of the driveway to find Rich's SUV parked behind my new car. When I enter the front door, I hear muffled voices. Approaching the kitchen, I see Rich on the patio, talking on the phone. While grabbing a bottle of water from the refrigerator, he turns and smiles in acknowledgement but continues to talk.

I take my water and go upstairs to change out of my suit. After kicking off my heels, I go to my dresser to grab a tank top. I'm taken aback when I see the battery of the TracFone sitting on top of the dresser. My heart stops beating and I begin to feel faint. What is it doing on my dresser? He must have found it on the floor and put it there for me see. Not knowing what to do, I remove my suit and blouse, and then quickly put my shirt and shorts on. I stand there, panicked and unable to move. What do I do with the battery? Does he want me to confront him with it?

I take a calming breath and hang my clothes up. Walking out of the bedroom, I pause, staring at the phone. If he didn't have the balls to confront me with it, then I won't either. I decide to leave it there. One of us will be forced to say something later, but I'm not in the mood for it right now. After turning off the light, I amble downstairs. Rich is sitting on the lounge chair by the pool, pressing keys on his phone. I pour myself a glass of wine and stand in the doorway, and he looks up at me.

"Hi."

"Hi. Have you been home a while?"

"Not too long. I picked us up some dinner. I need to get this email out, and then I'll be in."

Walking back into the kitchen, I notice that he brought home dinner from Alexander's—my favorite place in San Fran. He has to know about the phone. We never eat at, or order from, Alexander's unless it's a special occasion, and today certainly isn't anything exceptional. Frantic and unsure of what to do, I open the bag and take the food containers out, laying them on the counter with trembling hands. Opening up the cupboard to grab plates and silverware to set the table, I remember putting the last of the plates in the dishwasher this morning. I bend down and open it, only to find it's empty. A smile creeps on my face. Today is Monday, which means our housekeeper, Maria, was here. I bet she was the one that found the battery when she was sweeping the floor. Rich is still dressed in his suit, which likely means he hasn't even been upstairs yet.

I bustle upstairs and grab the battery from the dresser. Running across the bedroom, while practically tripping over my own feet, I shove it under the clothes with the other pieces of the phone. I make my way back downstairs to find Rich setting the table.

"Sorry to hear about your incident in court this morning. I know that there isn't much that I can do to cheer you up, but I hope this food can help turn your day around."

"Thanks. But yeah, I'd like to forget about this morning. I have a feeling it'll end up having many ramifications on my career. Thank you for dinner though. It's a sweet gesture."

We eat, while having our normal chatter of what the latest and greatest is at work, when out of the blue Rich asks, "Have you spoken to your mom?"

I look up, a bit taken aback by his question, since it seems unrelated to what we were talking about. "No, I haven't talked to her since Friday. I meant to call her back yesterday, but I never got a chance to. I didn't get to it today either."

"I stopped by her house today to get a copy of the itinerary for Thursday. I've also arranged to have a car pick us up that morning, to take us to the port."

"You're sure that you're able to come?"

"Yes. I moved a few appointments around to make it happen. I do think that I'll have to go to England shortly after we return though."

"Really? So, you're going to accept what they're proposing?"

"I don't have much of a choice. They're being pretty adamant about it. My hands are tied."

"What is it that they're propositioning?" I ask, putting my fork down on the plate. Looking up at him, I brace myself for the answer.

He slowly cuts a piece of steak, and then takes a bite. "They're building a new campus at one of their colleges," he responds, without looking me.

"Oh," I say, surprised by his reply. I was anticipating something else, recalling the—albeit one-sided—conversation that I overheard on Saturday. "That's not so bad."

"Yeah, I suppose."

We finish our dinner, and he announces that he has work to finish up, so he heads into the office, shutting the door behind him. I decide to put on my swimsuit and do a few laps in the pool.

When I'm done my swim, I take a shower. Rich is still in the office with the door closed so I decide to retire to the bedroom with a glass of wine and a book. I don't recall turning off the bedside light, but when I awake the bedroom is dark. Tugging the covers over me, I drift off to sleep.

The morning sun peaks through the shades. I stretch out on my back and take in a long breath. Please let today be better than yesterday. I decide to put on my new black Valentino sleeveless, couture dress, and then slip into my red Jimmy Choo gold studded stilettos. Today's a new day, and I'm going take it on in style.

chapter five

Tuesday
April 16, 2013
1:00 p.m.

"Sorry to interrupt. Amy, your one o'clock appointment is here," Julie announces, peeking her head into the conference room.

"Can you direct him into my office? I shouldn't be more than a few more minutes."

I conclude our staff meeting and congratulate Jackson on his win from yesterday. As I gather my things, my cell phone rings. It's my mom.

"Hi, Ames," she answers, her voice still sounding hoarse.

"Hi, Mom. Are you still sick?"

"Yeah. I'm fine though. I know you're busy, but I wanted to check in to see if you read the letter?"

My heart sinks to the pit of my stomach, and a big part of me regrets taking her call. "No, I haven't yet. Actually, I may have lost it. I swear it was in my purse, but when I returned from Catalina Island it was gone. I'll continue to look for it though. I'll find it."

"Oh... all right. I'll see you on Thursday morning then?" she asks after what seems like the longest pause in the history of pauses.

"Yes," I say, trying to sound overly excited, in an attempt to lighten the mood. "We'll be there. Rich said he got a copy of the itinerary. We plan to get there at least an hour before we need to board."

"Okay, sounds good, Ames. I'll let you get back to work. I love you, sweetie."

I gather my things and make my way toward my office. As I approach Julie's desk, she hurdles out of her chair. She hurries over to me, with the biggest grin on her face. "Wait until you see this guy," she says, fanning her face with her hand. "He's hot, Amy. Good luck trying to concentrate. Do you need me to come in and take notes for you?" She winks.

I laugh. "I think I can make do. It's evident that he's flustered you enough. I'm not sure you'd be much help at taking notes. That is, unless you're hungry for a bit of eye candy today."

She stares at me, wide-eyed and grinning. "Wait until you see him, you'll understand."

I look through the window of the office door. He stands next to my desk, with his back to us, looking out the window. "He doesn't look half bad from the back," I joke.

"Just you wait until you see his front."

I gasp, putting my hand up to my mouth. "Julie! I leave you alone with him for a couple of minutes and you've already explored his 'front?'" I quip, putting my fingers up displaying air quotes.

She slaps my arm. "I'm a married woman. You know what I meant. Get in there. Don't keep him waiting."

Grinning, I stroll to my office. I open the door slowly. "Sorry to keep you waiting," I say, stepping in and turning to close the door behind me.

When I turn back around, our eyes meet. Instantly, my legs become weak, my body starts to tingle, my eyes widen, and my breathing hitches. I step back, reaching for the door for support to hold me up. "Tra—"

He puts his hands into the pockets of his jeans, while looking intently into my eyes, not saying a single word.

My hand frantically searches for the door handle. "No," I mutter, barely able to speak. Finally finding my voice, "No!" I say louder. "No! No way! Nope. You need to get out." He freezes in place. Finding the doorknob, I turn it, swinging the door wide open behind me. "You need to get out now!" My entire body trembles. He doesn't move, and the look on his face is both terror and sadness.

"Please, Amy. Please," he says in a soft tone.

"I can't do this. I just can't do this right now. Please get out of my building, before I get someone to escort you out." He takes another step in my direction, while scanning the room behind me.

"I really... I need your help, Amy."

"No way. Nope. You don't need my help. I don't really know what the hell you're doing here, but you need to get out."

He bites down on his lower lip. "Amy, I don't know who to turn to. I really... really need your help."

"If the reason you're here is because you need a lawyer, well San Fran and all of California are full of them. Have your pick. But you don't need it to be me. If you need a referral, you can talk to Julie on your way out. Now please let me get on with my day."

He takes another couple steps toward me, putting his hands out like he's wanting to touch me. I take a step back. "No!"

Opening the door wider, I see a crowd of staff has formed. I scan the room. "Gus, Matthew, please show this guy the door." Stumbling out of my office, I walk on shaky legs to Julie's desk. Gus and Matthew rush toward my office.

"No need. I'm going," Travis says, with his head hanging low. He treads past me and mouths, "Sorry." I look away, and march back to my office.

After slamming the door behind me, I go over to the conference table, and with both hands I grab one of the three vases of roses. I chuck it as hard as my arms possibly can across the room, and watch it slam into the adjacent wall. Shattering in midair, water and glass goes flying everywhere. I grab the next vase on the table and throw that one in the same direction. It explodes into pieces as well. While getting ready to grab the last one, I feel a hand pull at my arm from behind.

"Don't, Amy," Julie advises. I was so focused in my fit of rage that I hadn't heard her come in. I lower my arms to my sides, and my entire body starts to shudder.

With her hand still on my arm, she pulls out a chair and directs me to sit. I lower myself into the chair while a sob forms. I cry. I rest my folded arms on the table and lower my head down onto them, and weep so hard that it rocks my entire body. Tears roll out of my eyes, down my face, and along my neck. Julie pulls a chair next to me, and leans in, rubbing my back. She sits silently, while I continue to cry for a long time.

When my tears cease forming, I sit with my head lowered on my arms, taking in slow breaths, attempting to calm myself. "I once loved him," I slur, between gasps, in a tone barely loud enough for anyone but myself.

"I'm sorry."

Raising my head from my arms, Julie offers me a tissue. "I loved him with every ounce of my being, and he tore up my world in return."

"I had no idea that you knew him when he called asking to meet with you. I'm so sorry, Amy. I would have never made the appointment, had I known."

"You couldn't have known," I respond, shaking my head. And it's that moment I'm reminded why he was here. My chest tightens. "It's his parents?"

"What?"

DECEPTION

"It's his parents. Someone killed his parents?" Somehow tears have found a way to form in my eyes again.

"Yeah."

There's a light knock at the door. It opens slightly, and Laura looks in. She enters the room, quietly shutting the door behind her. She comes to my side and stops when she sees the pool of water, glass, and roses covering the floor. Pulling a chair out on the other side of me, she sits, putting an arm around my shoulder. "I can't believe he had the nerve to show up here."

I stare at her and shake my head in disbelief. "Of all the law firms in the state, why does he think that I'm the best person to help him, after all that we've been through? Did he really think that I'm able to forget what he did to me?" I rest my head on her shoulder. "Did you hear? His parents were killed."

"I just heard about it. That's really sad."

Travis was once the love of my life. He was my entire world, until he decided to cheat on me and knock up some bimbo. We started dating when we were sophomores in high school, and our relationship grew until we became inseparable. We were excited when we both received our acceptance letters to Stanford. But then shortly afterward, Travis received notice that Yale was going to give him a full scholarship into the engineering program. He felt like he needed to take the scholarship; his parents weren't wealthy. They would be able to pay his loans while he was in school, but he would have had to take over payments once he graduated. That thought overwhelmed him. We made a pact that we would make it work; we convinced ourselves that our love was so strong that nothing could come between us. But six weeks after starting college, I got word that he was cheating on me. And the girl he was with was pregnant—three months pregnant. It shattered my world into a million pieces. I took the rest of the semester off and moved back home, spending every day lying in bed. My heart hurt so much that I decided I couldn't go on anymore, so I overdosed on my mom's prescription medication. After my mom found me unconscious, they had to revive me and pump the pills out of my system in the ER. It devastated my parents. I returned to school five months later and dedicated all of my time to studying, not giving a minute to any guy who happened to make advances. Beyond the initial phone calls, that went unanswered, I never heard from Travis again... until today. Seeing him in my office brought me back to that dark time in my life.

I convince Laura and Julie that I'll be fine—I'm really just wanting to be alone for a bit. After cleaning up the shattered glass and roses that blanket the floor, I throw it all in the trash. Why does every guy I give my heart to feel the need to cheat on me?

Deciding I need to get out of the office, I tell Julie that I'm leaving for the afternoon, and advise her to reschedule the rest of my meetings for the day. After lowering the roof on my convertible, I decide that I'm going to grab lunch and sit in the park. Immediately the thought of where I want to be sets in. I snatch my phone out of my purse and call Tracy. "Are you at work right now?"

"Yeah, I'm here, but just chatting with the girls. My last client left for the day. Why?"

"Will you come with me to the beach?"

"Oh—kay."

"I'll pick you up and explain on the way." I make a U-turn, heading back in the direction of her hair salon.

An hour later, we're being escorted to our table on the patio of the Love Shack. "Do you think he did it?" Tracy asks, sitting down at the table.

"I would like to think not, but I don't know. I haven't been in contact with him in over thirteen years.

I have no idea the person he's turned out to be, or what he's capable of." I shake my head.

"It was on the news last night. They were saying that one person is in custody, and they're questioning another. They never mentioned who it was, but it must be Travis and his brother," she says, with a concerned expression. "They mentioned that the victims were both stabbed multiple times. The police have the murder weapon. The news showed the house with police tape around it, and the cops were carrying out bags of evidence."

"I can't even wrap my mind around the fact that they're dead, Tracy. The thought that they were murdered makes my stomach hurt. They were such great people. I can't even think of anyone who would have wanted to harm them. I now regret not keeping in touch. They were like family to me. When Travis cheated on me, I couldn't get myself to talk to anyone in that family. I felt like they all betrayed me."

Our drinks arrive, and I down mine in one swift gulp before the waitress leaves.

"Can I get you another?" she asks, looking at me from the corner of her eye.

"Keep 'em coming."

"Not to change the subject, but did you ever find more out about Rich?"

"No. I haven't had much time alone the past couple days. He's been borderline sugary sweet, even bringing dinner home from Alexander's last night. He went over to my mom's to get the itinerary for the cruise on Thursday and scheduled a car to take us to the port in the morning," I say, with a quizzical look on my face. "I think Maria found the battery to the TracFone. It was sitting on my dresser when I got home from work yesterday."

"Are you sure it was her that found it? Could it have been Rich?"

"I thought the same thing too, but Maria was over yesterday. I know she swept and mopped the floors. Rich was still in his suit and showed no signs that he had been upstairs at all when I got home," I shrug. "If he was the one to find it, I think he would have confronted me with it."

"I'm not so sure of that, Amy," she says, furrowing her brow and shrugging. "So Rich is really going to take time off from work to go with you guys this weekend?"

"Yeah. I have to admit that I'm just as surprised. I can barely get him to spend a Friday evening with me, so I was certain he wasn't going. But he is."

"Hmm, interesting."

She stands, telling me that she has to go to the restroom. I sit, looking out at the ocean and attempt to push back the thought that Travis' parents were killed. It consumes me with complete sadness.

"Amy. Hello, Amy," Tracy says, waving a hand in front of my face. I look at her. "I've been trying to get your attention. What were you thinking about?"

"Sorry. I can't get the thought of Travis' parents out of my head. Not to mention, he's only thirty-two, and now has to live without his mom or dad. And his kid, or kids, since I don't even know how many he has now, lost their grandparents."

"Are you becoming soft, Amy?" she questions with a hint of concern. "Because I swear, during the entire ride here, you did nothing but curse his name repeatedly."

"Don't worry, I still want to curse his name. But his parents don't deserve what was done to them. And no child deserves to have their parents brutally ripped out of their lives."

"I know. So, what now?"

"What now?" I repeat. "Nothing. I go on the cruise with my family on Thursday. I'll figure out what to do about Rich when we get back. I refuse to leave it as it is. I need to know what exactly that TracFone is about, and if he's still cheating on me."

"And if he is?"

"Then I kick his ass to the curb, plain and simple. I'm a grown woman now. I refuse to let any man put me through all that again," I shoot back, raising my eyebrows, displaying confidence.

"I'll drink to that." She smiles. "Can you get the two grown women another round of drinks over here?" she says, putting her hand up to signal the waitress, who is now flirting with the bartender.

chapter six

Wednesday
April 17, 2013
4:52 p.m.

The workday passes quickly, not even having much time for lunch. I meet with the attorneys, making sure they have everything they need while I'm away. While looking at my email one last time, Laura walks in. She pulls out a chair and slumps down.

"So how was your meeting?"

She shrugs, looking unamused. "It went good. I always hate going to that place. I leave there feeling dirty." She tenses her shoulders and curls her lip in disgust.

DECEPTION

Laura had to meet with a client at the California State Prison in Los Angeles, and that place always leaves a woman feeling like a piece of meat.

"I know. I hate it too. The stares and nasty comments they yell out to the women in that place. Ugh," I say, looking equally disgusted. "So, when is the trial?"

"Not until the middle of June," she responds, standing. "You're leaving in the morning?"

"Yeah. I believe the car is picking us up around ten o'clock to take us to the port."

She nods once, and then simply stands there for a moment. "Have a good time," she says before the silence begins to feel uncomfortable.

"I will. It'll be nice to spend time with my family." She nods slightly again.

Walking to the door, she pauses after turning back in my direction. "Can we make time to talk when you get back?"

Pressing my lips together, I look up at her with a concerned face. "Yeah, sure. Is everything all right?"

She shrugs. "Of course it is. We haven't had much time to talk lately," she answers, with a forced smile.

"Are you sure that's all?"

"Yeah. Plus, I still haven't taken you out for your birthday."

"Okay," I say, still not really convinced that there isn't something she needs to talk to me about.

"Have a good time, Amy. I'll see you Monday."

She turns, and saunters out of the office, and I'm left feeling a bit unsettled and hoping that she doesn't want to leave the firm because of what happened in court on Monday. She's always hard on herself, so much more than even I am.

My phone dings just as I'm turning off the computer. A text from Rich: *Need to work a bit later tonight to finish up some things, since I'll be gone for a few days. Don't wait for me for dinner. I'll grab something quick at work.*

"Whatever," I say under my breath. I grab my bag and keys, and turn the lights off, closing the door behind me. "What are you still doing here?"

"I'm finishing up a few last-minute things," Julie responds, typing.

"Get home. That can wait until tomorrow. Come on, we'll walk out together."

She smiles, and finishes up, before turning off her computer.

DECEPTION

I spend the next few hours packing my suitcase—stuffing enough clothes for a month-long vacation. Realizing I should pack a couple of sweaters, since it may be cold in the evenings on the ship, I go to my closet and reach up on the shelf. While grabbing a sweater, the pieces of the TracFone fall to the floor. The sickening feeling in the pit of my stomach returns. I pick the pieces up and shove them back under the clothes on the shelf. While adding the sweaters to the stack in the suitcase, I look over at the clock and see that it's ten-twenty-five.

I decide to get in the shower and call it a night. Upon getting out of the shower, footsteps approach on the stairs. And while bushing my hair, Rich peeks into the bathroom.

"Hi."

"Hey."

"Did you pack?"

"Yeah, I think I have everything."

"I guess it's my turn then," he says, walking to the closet.

"What time is the car coming to pick us up in the morning?" I inquire, peering out of the bathroom while brushing my teeth.

"Ten-forty-five."

"That late?"

"Yeah. We can't board until eleven-thirty."

I finish up in the bathroom and lay in bed while watching Rich pack.

I must have fallen asleep because I awake to him shutting off the bedroom light. I close my eyes and resume my sleep.

chapter seven

Thursday
April 18, 2013
10:37 a.m.

My phone chimes. It's a text from my mom: *Call me when you get here, and we'll meet up.*

I respond: *Okay, see you soon.*

I put the phone in the front pocket of the suitcase. Rich is in the office, typing on the computer, so I drag our bags downstairs from the bedroom. I set them outside on the porch.

He strolls out the office. "The car is going to be a bit late. Mark called saying that there's some kind of accident on the highway, and traffic is backed up."

"How late?"

He shrugs, looking unconcerned. "He said ten or fifteen minutes."

Feeling frustrated, I plop myself down on the top step. The minutes feel like hours. Finally at eleven-ten, Mark pulls up. "He's here," I call to Rich.

He comes out and locks the door to the house. Mark meets us to take our bags. Not apologizing for being late, he puts our suitcases in the trunk of the car and opens the back door for me.

On our way, I keep glancing at my watch. It feels like forever. "Doesn't he know we're running late," I remark to Rich, under my breath. He shrugs.

Finally, we arrive at the port. I note that it's eleven-forty-eight. At least we still have time. Mark takes our bags out of the trunk, while Rich walks over to the check-in booth. Taking my phone out of the suitcase, I see that I have two missed calls and four text messages. "What the hell?"

I open up the first text message, received at ten-forty-one. It's from my brother: *Where are you?*

The next text message is from my mom, received at ten-fifty-two: *Amy, answer your phone. We're boarding right now. Where are you guys? Call me when you get here.*

DECEPTION

The next message is from my brother, at eleven-twenty-two: *Are you guys all right? We're getting worried.*

And the last message is from my mom, at eleven-thirty-four: *Amy, what happened? The ship is backing out of the port. We tried to have them wait, but they said that they couldn't.*

I dart over to Rich. "The ship left?" I ask, exasperated.

"I guess. I... I thought that it wasn't leaving until twelve-thirty. Apparently, I read the itinerary wrong. I thought it said we could board at eleven-thirty, but it says that the ship leaves at that time." I stand there flabbergasted, looking at him with a shocked look, my mouth hanging open. "So, what now?"

"They said that they can try to get us on the next ship that is scheduled to leave today at five-forty-five."

"I don't want to go on the other cruise," I yell. "My family is on this cruise."

"I know, Amy. I'm sorry," he says, wrapping his arm around me. "I fucked up. I'm sorry."

"Take me home," I direct, wiggling out of his arms.

I snatch my phone out of my pocket, and text my mom: *Sorry, we didn't make it in time. Rich is an asshole.*

"Amy?" Julie says, confused, when she sees me walk in. "What are you doing here?" She gives me a once over, looking at my sundress and sandals.

"Don't ask, Julie. Long story. I'm forced to stay home." I stomp to my office, and Julie follows directly behind.

"You're not going?"

"We got to the port after the ship had already left. My family was forced to go without me."

"Are you serious, Amy? How late were you?"

"We got there about eleven-fifty. The ship pulled out of port around eleven-thirty," I answer, pushing my lips together in a tight line, and raising my eyebrows in annoyance.

"Why did it take you guys so long to get there?"

"Well, Rich thought that we were supposed to board at eleven-thirty, so he scheduled a car to pick us up for ten-forty-five. The car got there late because of an accident or something. I think we would've been late to board, regardless, because the ship was scheduled to leave at eleven-thirty."

"No wait, you mean the car was scheduled to pick you up at nine-forty-five, right?"

"No, ten-forty-five, because he thought we were boarding at eleven-thirty." I shoot her a quizzical look.

"Well, when Rich called here on Monday looking for you, he asked me if I had the itinerary. I told him I did. He asked me to email a copy to him. He also asked me to schedule a car service to take you to the port. When he asked me what time you needed to be there, I told him you could board at ten-thirty. He said to schedule the car to be at your house for nine-forty-five. I know I told the woman on the phone to have the car at your house by that time. I received the invoice this morning in the mail, and it clearly states nine-forty-five on it."

"What? Why? What?"

"I don't know, Amy. But I'm not lying. Do you want to see the invoice?"

"I believe you. But I don't understand what happened."

"Maybe Rich looked at the itinerary afterward and thought that I got the time wrong, so he called to reschedule the car service?" she says, shrugging.

I narrow my eyes, not really convinced. "Maybe."

"That really sucks, Amy. Your mom was looking forward to this."

"I know. And so was I."

"Are you really here to work? You should go somewhere else for the weekend."

"No. The only place I want to be right now is with my family on that cruise. And I can't. I'm here to work," I say, annoyed. "And I certainly don't want to be home with him right now," I mutter under my breath. She frowns. I shrug.

I tell her that I'm going to close the door and catch up on some work and advise her to not let anyone know that I'm here. Taking out my iPod, I place the ear buds in my ears and look through case files. But I can't seem to stay focused. I toss my sandals off and put my feet up on the desk. Leaning back in the chair, I close my eyes and allow myself to get lost in the music. Reflecting on my life, thoughts of Travis' parents consume me. Feeling guilty for blowing up at him yesterday, I think about how alone he must feel not having his parents anymore. Then suddenly, thoughts of everything that he put me through fill my head, and I'm left unsure of what the right thing is to do.

I page Julie. "Do you have a phone number for Travis Cashman?" I ask her while she stands in the doorway.

"The guy that you kicked out of here yesterday? Your ex?" she questions, wide-eyed.

"Yes," I respond, trying to look confident.

DECEPTION

"I believe that he left his number when he called to make the appointment."

"Can you call him to see if he's still interested in speaking with me?"

"Are you sure about that, Amy?" she asks, searching my face for an expression.

"Yes. Please."

"I'll call him now. Do you want to meet with him today?"

"Yes. Whatever time he can come in," I respond, straight-faced.

A few minutes later she comes back. "I spoke with him. He said that he can be here within the hour."

"Thank you, Julie. Let me know when he gets here." She nods, not so confidently, and shuts the door behind her. I replace the ear buds in my ears, and turn up the music, while staring out the window at the clouds.

❁

Julie pulls one of the ear buds out. I'm startled. "Sorry. I tried calling to you from the door, but I don't think you heard me."

"It's okay."

"Mr. Cashman is here," she announces, motioning in the direction of the door.

I spin the chair around, and gaze at Travis. He has a small smirk on his face and it sends chills down my spine. He shuffles from one foot to the other, appearing unsure. Swallowing hard, I bend down, putting my sandals on. Julie hustles out, and I get up from the chair.

"Come have a seat," I say, directing him to sit at the table.

Hesitantly, he pulls a chair out and sits down. He folds his hands together on the table and looks down at them. I sit at the opposite side and open my notebook. When I place the audio recorder in the middle of the table, he looks at what I'm doing through his eyelashes. The silence is deafening.

Clearing my throat, I look directly at him. "I want to make one thing clear to you. I didn't ask you here to talk about us," I say, waving a hand in the air, gesturing between us. "I don't want to talk about our past—" He raises his head and opens his mouth to speak, but I quickly intercept him by raising my finger for him to wait. "Please. Let me talk Travis." He retreats, lowering his head back down, but this time, he keeps his eyes fixed on mine. Sadness overwhelms his expression. "I'm willing to assist you and your brother, if it'll help find who killed your parents. I only want to talk about this case and, after we're done you'll go on living your life as will I. Get it?"

"Yes."

"If you're sure that this is what you want, then I agree to help. I'll be asking you a lot of questions. Some of them will be difficult, considering what happened to your parents. Please know, everything I ask you is in an attempt to uncover the truth, and hopefully create a clear case to eliminate you as a suspect. I don't represent individuals who I believe are not innocent. I don't feel right allowing innocent people to sit behind bars, but I also don't allow guilty ones to walk the streets on my watch. If, at any time, I believe that you're guilty, I will demand that you seek other representation. Is that clear?"

"Yes."

"I'll interview you today and call over to the jail to schedule a time to meet with your brother, Brian, tomorrow."

"You don't need to do that." He shakes his head.

"What do you mean? Does your brother already have a lawyer?"

"Yes. He does."

"So why are you guys seeking separate council?" I ask, skeptical.

"He's hired his friend, who is a low life attorney, and I'm not certain that he's the right lawyer to have. He runs with the same crowd as Brian. I don't want to be associated with that," he says, before pausing. "And I'm not sure if my brother is innocent."

"Do you think that your brother is capable of killing your parents?" I ask, shocked by his honesty.

"When he's high on meth," Travis says, shrugging, "anything is possible." He looks straight into my eyes and it feels like he's peering into my soul. I have to look away. His smoky, gray blue eyes that are filled with so much sorrow make me feel like breaking down the wall that I want so desperately to have between us—the same wall that I built up thirteen years ago, when I lost the one person who I thought was my soul mate.

"Is it all right if I record our interview?"

"Yes."

I press the record button and begin. "Let's start off with you telling me a bit more about your parents." Travis raises his head and furrows his brow. "I know... I mean, I know who your parents are, but I need to know more about their life for the past year or so," I quickly elaborate. He nods. "So, your parents were living in Half Moon?"

"Yes. They moved from San Francisco about three years ago."

DECEPTION

"What was the reason for their move?"

"They were planning for retirement. Their old house was much too large for them, and they wanted to move closer to their granddaughter."

"They have one granddaughter? Your daughter?"

"Yes. Amanda," he replies, nodding. My cell phone rings. I ignore it.

"Were your parents still working?"

"Yes. My dad had moved his garage to Half Moon, and my mom transferred to the elementary school there. She was planning on retiring at the end of the school year."

"So, they lived a pretty quiet life?"

He shrugs, but keeps his gaze directly on mine, making me shift in my chair and want to look away. "Mostly. When my brother was clean, things seemed normal. But he's been in and out of rehab for the past eight or so years. Every time he'd come out, they would offer him a place to stay. He'd stay clean for a bit, but it never lasts long. It caused a lot of stress for my parents. It was a never-ending cycle. Each time he'd fall back into his old ways, I could see my mom place guilt on herself. She always felt guilty for his bad decisions. I never really understood why." He clears his throat, looking away. I can see the sadness on his face build up.

"Would you like a glass of water?" He shakes his head. My cell phone rings again. "Sorry about that," I say, my phone chiming again. "Let me turn that off," I add, getting up and sauntering over to my desk.

Before pressing the power button, I see a text from Rich: *Why aren't you answering your phone?*

I text back: *Stop calling. I'm at work and busy.*

While I want to chuck the phone across the room, I quickly remember that Travis is sitting not five feet away from me, and I already scared him off yesterday. I press the power button—quite hard—to power it down, and then shove it into the bottom of my purse. I huff loudly, returning to the table.

"Was your brother living with your parents at the time of their death?" I continue.

"Yes. He just came out of rehab the week prior," Travis says in a slow, controlled voice, that I'm now realizing he's had the entire time he's been here.

"And you and your family live in Half Moon as well?"

"No. I live and work in Pescadero." I nod, not ever having been to Pescadero, or even knowing where it is.

"All right, so now I need to know, in detail, what you did on Friday. I'll need for you to try to remember everything, including the time that you did it, from the moment you woke up to the moment you went to bed.

DECEPTION

If you can't recall something, we can skip over it for now. But I really need for you to try to remember as much as possible. I'll make a timeline while you tell me the details."

"Okay," he responds, shifting in his chair. I note that this is the first time he's done this since he sat down.

"So run through your day, starting with the time you woke up."

"I woke up at six-fifteen and got Amanda up at six-thirty. I cooked her breakfast, and then dropped her off at school at seven-forty-five. I drove to work and was there until two o'clock. Amanda stayed after school for computer club, so I drove to the school to pick her up at two-fifteen. We then went to the bakery down the street to pick up a cake for my parents. It was my parents' thirty-seventh wedding anniversary. After, we drove to Half Moon and stopped at a local florist. Amanda wanted to get her grandma some flowers. We also picked up some take-out from my parent's favorite restaurant."

"What time did you get to Half Moon?" I interrupt.

He shrugs. "I think it was around three o'clock, or so."

"Okay. Continue," I instruct, putting my pen back to the paper.

"So, we went over to my parents' house. My mom had just gotten home from work. My dad was in the garage, working on a car. And Brian was out somewhere. I texted him to see if he was going to join us, and he texted back saying he'd be over in fifteen minutes. When he got there, we all sat down and ate. Amanda was going over to a friend's house for a sleepover, so we left."

"What time was that?"

He pauses in thought, and then he presses his lips together and lightly shakes his head. "I think it was around four-thirty."

"All right."

"Brian wanted to go out, so he asked me for a ride. He had me drop him off at a friend's house about three or so miles away. Then Amanda and I drove back home. She packed an overnight bag, and I drove her to her friend's house."

"Do you recall what time you dropped her off?"

"I remember it was just before five o'clock, because her friend's parents asked me if I wanted to stay for dinner. I recall looking at the time. I couldn't stay because I had to return to work."

"So, you went straight to work after dropping your daughter off at her friend's house?"

He looks down at his hands. "No, actually, I went home for a bit. I needed to shower."

"What time did you get to work?"

"I think it was around seven o'clock."

"And what time were you at work until?"

He swallows hard and takes a deep breath. "Until my brother called saying that my parents were—" He takes a moment to clear his throat, and then says softly adds, "—dead."

My breathing quickens and tears prickle in the back of my eyes. "And do you remember what time that was?"

"I remember it exactly, it was eight-forty-one," he answers, trying to look composed.

"Do you need a break?" I ask him, hoping he'll say yes since I could certainly use one.

"No, I'm fine."

"This is where it'll get hard. I understand if you have a difficult time answering some of this. But please know, I'm asking so that I can understand everything that happened. I will get police reports, but I do need for you to tell me what you know." I want so badly to reach my hand across the table and touch his arm. I refrain and put my pen back to the paper instead.

"How were your parents killed?" I ask, forcing out each word.

He looks down. "They were stabbed repeatedly. They each had over twenty wounds to the chest, and my dad's neck was also sliced open."

"Did it appear as they fought back?" I manage.

I see a tear roll down his cheek, but he doesn't attempt to wipe it away. "My mom was bound to a kitchen chair, her legs and hands were both tied. My dad was found on the floor next to her. I don't know if they fought back."

No longer able to hold back, I reach my hand across the table and touch his forearm. He flinches for a moment, but then looks up at me and tears stream down his face. He continues looking into my eyes while the tears flow. I can't hold back my own tears anymore. I, too, let it out.

"I miss them Amy," he says tenderly.

"I know."

Even knowing what it's like to lose a parent, I can't begin to understand how it is to lose both parents in such a tragic way. "I think this is enough for today," I say, keeping my eyes fixed on his. He looks sad, tired, and broken. "If the police or any reporters ask to speak with you, please tell them to contact me. I don't want you talking to any of them without me there."

I turn off the audio recorder. He nods quickly, wiping the tears from his face. "I'll need more information from you in the next few days. I may even need to speak with anyone you were with that day to corroborate your story, in case we should end up needing it. That might include having to speak with your daughter, your wife, and coworkers."

He shakes his head. "There's no wife, it's just me and Amanda." No wife? He must be divorced. A few years back, I heard that he was married.

"How old is your daughter? Do you think she'll be fine to answer some questions?" I ask, already anticipating the answer.

"Amanda's thirteen. And yes, she'd be fine to answer questions."

"By the way, why is your brother in custody?" I probe, remembering that I don't know the reason.

"His fingerprints were on the bloody knife they found."

I bite down on my lower lip. "All right. Well, in the meantime, please try to think of any reason why someone would do this to your parents, including your brother. Try to remember anything that will help us to get the justice that they deserve." I stand. "Call me with any information."

"I will," he responds, pushing in his chair. We stand in silence for a moment, and then he smiles ever-so-slightly. "Thank you Amy. Thank you." His beautiful smile sends my pulse racing. I look down at the floor briefly.

"You're welcome Travis. They were once my family too," I manage to force out, choking back tears.

He shuffles to the door. And not wanting him to go yet, I decide to walk him out. Once we reach the lobby, he pauses and then turns. He leans in to hug me.

Before I can think, I wrap both arms around his shoulders. "Everything will be okay," I say calmly.

Before I pull away, I take in a breath and his scent intoxicates me. I'm instantly reminded of us—of our past—and of the times that I was so madly in love with him. When we let go, I feel like pulling him back in and smelling him some more. But I think better of it.

He pushes the door open, without looking away from me. He hesitantly turns and disappears. I remain standing in place a moment longer, absorbing the lingering scent of him in the air. Once my legs begin to feel weak, I return to my office and Julie trails behind. "So how did it go?"

I smile somewhat, but it fades quickly, replaced with sadness. "It was fine. It was difficult, but it went well. We didn't finish the interview. It was too much for one day."

She can see the sorrow on my face, so she nods. "Rich was here. When I told him that you were in a meeting with a client, he said he would wait. But then he took a phone call and decided to leave."

"You didn't tell him who I was meeting with, did you?"

She chuckles. "No. I was not going there with him after the morning you've had."

"Good. Thank you."

I tell her that I'm going to leave for the day since I don't have any other appointments scheduled. "Do you have a copy of that invoice we spoke about this morning?" I ask her on my way out.

"It's right here," she says, handing it to me.

"Thank you, Julie. I'll be in tomorrow. See you then."

I decide it's time to go home and confront Rich with the invoice.

Where the hell is he? I pace the floor and glare out the window. I haven't been able to do anything but pace the floor of the entire house since getting home nearly four hours ago.

I decide to text him before I burn a hole directly into the floorboards. *Where are you?* I text, and then put the phone in my pocket.

ISABELLE VAN BUREN

After ten minutes of more pacing, my feet start to ache so I sit on the arm of the couch, resting my feet on the cushion, while staring out the window.

Another hour passes, and still no sign of Rich. "If he's not going to come to me, then I guess I need to go to him," I rage, grabbing my keys, and storming out the door.

I drive to the one place I hope he'll be—his office. I pass by slowly, attempting to see if there are any lights on. But I don't see any. I drive to the back of the building, and find his car in the parking lot, along with another car as well. I've seen that other car before, but don't recall who it belongs to. What do I do now? Do I attempt to text him again, or do I go into his office? What if he's with a client, and I go storming in with the invoice in hand? I'm torn, so I sit a while longer running through a variety of scenarios.

Moments later, I turn the engine off, grab my phone, and walk to the front door. It's locked, so I press my face up against the dark windows and peer in, looking toward his office. I can see a dim light. Remembering that I have a spare key, I slide it into the keyhole. Should I go in? My conscience says no, but I eventually say screw it.

I open the door and walk into the lobby. It's quiet. But as I stand there, listening for voices, I can hear muffled sounds coming from behind Rich's closed office door. I take slow steps in that direction, keeping in mind that he doesn't like to be interrupted when he's in a meeting.

When I get to his office, I look into the long narrow window beside the door, and I gasp. Afraid that he's heard me, I put my hand over my mouth while I let out an even louder gasp. I'm motionless and unsure of what to do next. In the faint light, Rich leans back against his desk. He appears to be completely naked. A girl is kneeling down in front of him and she seems to be wearing something. I narrow my eyes, because while it looks like it's a dress, it also doesn't look like any dress I've ever seen. She's draped in black leather something-or-other, with chains hanging off of it everywhere. Her hands are behind her back, and they're bound by something that look like handcuffs or chains?

I jump in response to a loud whooshing sound, and then gut-wrenching screams. Rich has a whip in his hand and he's flogging her backside with it. She lets out a scream with every crack of the whip. But, then she quickly continues to provide him with oral satisfaction. What the hell is going on?

Adrenaline kicks in. I throw open the door, but neither one of them hear me since Rich just whipped her again. Her shrieks fill the room. He throws his head back in gratification. I instinctively snap a picture with my phone. When the flash illuminates the room, Rich turns his head in my direction. The girl removes her mouth from his midsection and darts her head toward me.

My mouth drops open. I know her. "How dare you?" I retort, so angry that I'm surprised to be able to speak.

Not wanting to be there a moment longer, I dash out of his office. "Amy. Don't—" Rich calls out. But I don't care to hear what he has to say.

I start breathing hard, and my chest tightens, while I try to I hold back tears. I feel like I'm either going to be sick or punch a hole in the wall. I do neither. I stomp out the door and run to my car. With my hands shaking uncontrollably, I glare over at the car that I recognized. It's Sarah, my best friend, Laura's sister. The same Sarah that Laura told me on Sunday was pregnant.

I put the key in the ignition and stomp on the gas pedal, sending the tires squealing out of the parking lot. I drive straight home, struggling to remain focused on the speed limit and traffic lights.

I march upstairs to the bedroom, go to my closet, and gather all of the pieces of the TracFone. Marching over to his side of the bed, I throw it on top of his pillow. Heading back downstairs, I take hold of the handle to my suitcase that's still packed for my trip. I stroll out the door and get in my car. My phone dings as I back out of the driveway. Without looking down at it, I press the power button and toss it onto the seat next to me.

I drive headed nowhere. My body feels numb—no tears are to be formed, no sadness is to be felt, and no anger is to be expressed. I need to call Laura. I need to talk to someone. If she knows about this and didn't tell me, that might devastate me more than what I just witnessed.

Deciding that I need to be alone with my thoughts for a while, I do the first thing that comes to mind, I check into a hotel. I draw the curtains, and curl up into a ball in the middle of the bed and allow the numbness that I was feeling to subside. Instantly, all of the emotions of sadness and anger ravage me.

chapter eight

Friday
April 19, 2013
9:35 a.m.

After completely losing myself in my fit of rage last night, sleep finally found me around four o'clock this morning. It must have been quite the hard sleep because I woke up with my mind clear, body refreshed, and sadness gone. I've always considered myself a strong woman—I've had to be with everything I went through after what Travis did to me at such a young age. But today, I feel better than I have in quite some time. Maybe catching Rich in the act was exactly what I needed to stop fooling myself into believing that our relationship was strong. As I sit here in this hotel room this morning, it's clear to me that I was in denial. No man would ever continually put their work before the love of their life. I might not be made for a serious relationship, I need to accept that—I will accept that. I spent six years after the situation with Travis without a man by my side. Rich appeared out of nowhere, like a knight on a white horse, ready to save me from the demons of the world. But now, I realize that I might've been color blind. He's certainly no knight, and his horse is certainly black like his heart.

I don't feel like speaking to anyone today. I need to figure what to do next. But I have to at least call Julie to let her know I won't be coming in. After turning on my cell phone, it vibrates and displays that I have nine voicemail messages. I shake my head, refusing to listen to them. I press four, and wait for her to pick up.

"Are you all right?" Julie answers, with concern in her voice.

"Yes, I'm fine. Why do you ask?" I respond, wondering how she even knows that something is up.

"Rich is looking for you. He was parked outside when I got to work at eight o'clock. He asked me if I had heard from you. He stayed out there until about nine-fifteen. What's going on?"

"I need some time to myself. I have things to sort through. I won't be at work today, but I'm fine."

"Your mom called this morning as well. She said you weren't home or answering your phone."

"My mom?"

"Yeah. She said that she was worried about you. She didn't know if something had happened to you because you never showed up yesterday morning. She took the first flight home, as soon as the ship docked."

"Did you tell her that we had arrived late?" I ask her, panicked that my mom is so worried.

"I did. But, Amy, she didn't sound like she believed me."

"I'll call her."

"Please tell me that you're okay. You'd tell me if you weren't, right?"

"I'm fine, Julie, I promise," I reassure her. "Can you tell Laura to call me as soon as she gets in?"

"Sure."

"Thank you. If Rich happens to show up there again, please tell him I'm not going to be in today, and to leave the building. Get Gus or Matthew to escort him out, if you should need it."

"Okay. But you're really worrying me."

"Don't worry, Julie, everything will be fine."

DECEPTION

I set my phone down on the nightstand and not a minute later it chimes. Looking down at it, I anticipate it being a text from my mom. Instead, it's from Rich: *We need to talk.*

I roll the phone in my hands contemplating if I want to respond.

I text back: *We don't need to talk. Nothing you could say to me would matter right now.*

My phone dings again: *Please, Amy. You need to give me the opportunity to explain.*

I respond: *There is no explanation that will make a difference. I don't want to hear you try to justify how having your dick in another woman's mouth while you whip her brings you satisfaction. Or how you spent Valentine's Day christening another woman's sofa. I also don't care to listen to you explain how you never wanted children with me, but you get another woman pregnant. I'm not what you want, it's very apparent. You are better off walking away.*

I toss the phone onto the bed, deciding that was the last communication I will have with that lying, cheating bastard. I elect to take a shower, and then I'll call my mom.

When I exit the bathroom, I hear my phone ring. While not caring to look at who could be calling, something makes me look at it anyway. It's actually not Rich calling, it's Julie.

"Hi, Julie. Is everything all right there?"

"Yes. He hasn't returned. But Travis called a couple of minutes ago, saying that he needs to speak with you. I told him you weren't in today. But he said that he really needed to talk with you today. I didn't know what to tell him, so I said I would relay the message to you."

"Damn it. I forgot that I told him we would meet again. But today is not a good day for it."

"He really sounded desperate. Something in his voice made it appear like he had something important to tell you."

"Do you have his phone number?"

I stare down at the number for a while, trying to decide if I'm in the right frame of mind to do this today. Huffing loudly, I press the numbers into the keypad and wait. The line rings repeatedly, and eventually his voicemail picks up. My breath quickens at the sound of his voice. I immediately hang up.

Instead of leaving a message, I decide to text him: *It's Amy. My assistant told me you wanted to talk. I'm busy today, but we can schedule a meeting for Monday, if that's okay.*

I hover my finger over the Send button, and then after a few seconds gently press it.

I dry off my hair and sit on the bed, getting ready to call my mom when my phone chimes.

Travis: *I really need to speak with you today. Not sure if I can wait until Monday to tell you what I need to. Can we please meet up today?*

I sigh. I really don't think I can deal with work today, but I also know that he might need to get all of the information together as soon as possible. I call instead of texting him again.

"Hi," he answers, and my stomach flutters with that one word.

"Hi," I respond, before reminding myself why I called him. "I know I said we needed to meet again, but I'm busy today. Can we schedule to meet first thing on Monday morning?" I hear him breath into the phone and it sends chills throughout my body.

"I really need to talk to you today. I can't go another day without telling you something." His response makes me think he wants to talk about something other than his parents.

"Travis, if what you have to say to me has anything to do with our past, then I don't want to hear it. I told you yesterday that I don't want to talk about that."

"Amy, I wasn't completely honest with you yesterday. I... can't go another day without telling you the truth."

Suddenly, I feel anger simmer. "Travis, I told you yesterday that I needed you to be completely honest with me. If you are now saying that you weren't, I don't think I want to help you. And if you had anything—anything at all—to do with your parents' death, I suggest that you turn yourself in right now," I say, my voice rising with every word.

"No, Amy. No. I promise I didn't kill my parents. I really need to clarify something that I said yesterday, I need for you to know. Please give me a couple minutes of your time today. I promise that's all I want."

I close my eyes and attempt to calm myself from the fury that I'm experiencing. "Okay, Travis. I will give you a couple minutes to explain yourself. But you better understand, if this is some kind of hoax to get me to believe a lie, I will find out. I've had my share of dealing with lies. I refuse to help you if you continue to do so." He's silent. "What time can you meet?" I ask, with a hint of annoyance in my voice.

"Can we meet this morning?"

"Meet me in the lobby of The Clift hotel at eleven o'clock."

"The Clift? All right."

"See you then," I say, hanging up.

My phone dings again; it's a text from Rich. I decide not to even look at it. Instead, I dial my mom's number.

"Amy," she answers, and I notice her voice is still rough.

"Mom? You still don't sound well. Are you feeling okay?"

"Amy, I was so worried about you. I couldn't stay on vacation. I had to come and see if you were all right," she says in a hushed tone, barely sounding like my mom.

"You didn't have to leave in the middle of your vacation. You should've stayed."

"Honey, I really needed to know that you were fine. And I need to speak with you," she says hesitantly.

"Is everything okay? You're starting to scare me."

She sighs, and then I hear her take in a breath. "Everything will be fine. But I don't want to do this over the phone. I really need to speak with you in person."

"I can come over. Just give me a few—" I say, suddenly remembering that I'm meeting with Travis in less than an hour. "Um, can I come over after lunch? Is that soon enough?"

"Yes, Ames, that's perfect. Please know that I love you."

"Mom, you're scaring me."

"Honey, I love you and everything will be all right. I promise." I nod, knowing she can't see me, but I can't find my voice.

I sit in the restaurant off of the lobby in the hotel, sipping on water and staring at the door. After what feels like forever, Travis appears. Standing at the entryway, he scans the lobby. I stand up from my chair and wave my hand to catch his attention. He looks in my direction and makes his way to me. I sit back down without saying anything.

Pulling the chair out on the other side of the table, he sits. He nods his head slightly, seeming like he's giving himself an internal pep talk. I look at him with mixed emotion—a part of me is not wanting to hear what he's about to say, another part of me is angry that he wasn't completely honest with me yesterday, and a small—albeit significant—part of me is downright drawn to him. I try not to show any emotions. While I try and quiet the many voices in my head, I'm outright gushing over this gorgeous man with gray blue eyes, tousled, light brown hair, well-groomed scruff, and lips that I can't seem to move my eyes away from. The voice of reason abruptly screams out, awakening me from my trance, reminding me why he's even here right now.

"I've been tearing myself up all night because I wasn't completely truthful with you yesterday. Uh—" he says, finally breaking the silence. He looks down and swallows hard. "I didn't go home after dropping Amanda off at her friend's house the evening that my parents were killed. I actually drove to San Francisco to drop something off, and then I immediately drove back. I did get to work until just after seven o'clock."

Not understanding why he wouldn't have told me this yesterday, I narrow my eyes while stretching my head forward to get him to look up at me. "I'm confused as to why you didn't tell me this yesterday. Why did you say you went home?"

Biting down on his lower lip, he raises his head and looks straight into my eyes. "The thing I had to drop off was—" He takes a moment to swallow, still holding his gaze on mine. "I was at your office," he finishes. Immediately, it all becomes clear to me.

"The sunflower?" I manage to inquire. He doesn't respond. "They were from you? But why?" I ask, shaking my head, confused. "Why after all these years, Travis?"

"I think you need to talk to your mom."

"My mom?" I shoot him a muddled look. "What does this have to do with my mom?"

"Amy, I promise that she'll be able to explain it to you."

I rub my hands over my face, feeling completely staggered and hoping that I'll wake up at any moment with this being a horrid dream. "Was your parents' death an elaborate scheme to get me to talk to you?" I shoot back, really not sure where that question is coming from. I know that it makes no sense what-so-ever, but I'm so confused right now that I can't even think straight.

"No. Of course not. No. Why would you think that?" he asks, sounding disgusted by my question.

"I know, I'm sorry," I say, shaking my head. "You have to understand that none of this makes sense to me, so I'm left unsure of what to think."

He reaches across the table and puts his fingers under my chin, pushing it up so that our eyes meet. The touch of his hand on my face sends my heart nearly into cardiac arrest, and I find myself having to catch my breath.

"Please believe me when I say that I had nothing to do with my parents' death. I wasn't honest with you yesterday because I was afraid to tell you I was here. I couldn't go another day without telling you the truth

DECEPTION

though. I don't want to lie to you. I want you to know the truth."

"The truth about what?"

"I don't think it's my place to tell you, Amy. I mean, I could tell you, but your mom is really the one that needs to explain everything to you. Please know that it all comes from a good place. You deserve to know the truth. You've been lied to for too long."

I close my eyes, feeling the room spin around me. I've been lied to for too long? What is that supposed to mean? Was everyone in on Rich's betrayal? Is that what he's referring to?

Travis stands and extends his hand. I hesitate. "I think I'm going to stay here for a bit," I say, not able to move. He nods, and then offers an endearing smile. It comforts me ever-so-slightly.

He walks away, leaving me confused and scared.

My phone rings. Seeing that it's Rich calling, I power my phone off and ring the doorbell.

"Amy, I'm so happy you're here," my mom greets me. She draws me in for a long hug. It feels good. "Let's go sit outside in the backyard," she says, leading me through the kitchen. Pausing at the counter, she takes a stack of folders into her arms and walks outside with me following behind.

I sit at the table on the patio and fold my hands into my lap. My heart is beating out of my chest, feeling like I may pass out. I'm not sure if I even want to hear what she has to say. My life is headed down a road that I don't want to go down.

She pulls her chair up next to mine, and puts an arm around my shoulder, pulling me in toward her. "Ames, you look terrified. Don't be, honey. Everything will be fine. I really need for you to know a few things." She pauses, clearing her throat. "I'm struggling to figure out where to begin. I don't even understand it all myself."

I look at her, scared of what she's about to say. "Mom, please tell me."

She nods. "Okay." She opens the folder on the top of the stack. "I will start from the beginning," she says, handing me a sheet of paper.

I scan it. It's a letter from Yale University, dated March 24, 2000, addressed to Travis. It's the letter he received in the mail notifying him of his academic scholarship. I narrow my eyes, looking up from the letter, "Oh—Kay?" I know there has to be more to this.

She hands me a stack of papers, stapled together. The page on top is an invoice from Yale University in the amount of $27,043. I flip to the second page, which is a copy of a check for that same amount to Yale University, from Warren Silver Law Associates, my dad's law firm. The last page is an email correspondence from my dad to Roger, the accountant. I read it under my breath: *"Roger, please pay this invoice that I've attached. This amount is to cover the first semester of Travis Cashman's schooling, as we discussed last week. Please mail the check directly to Yale University."* I shake my head, feeling even more confused than ever.

"Dad paid for Travis to go to college?"

"Yes, apparently your dad paid for Travis to go to Yale. There was no academic scholarship." She lays her hand on the stack of folders. "I could have you sit here and read all of these, but I think it's easier for me to tell you what I know."

"All right."

"Two weeks before your dad passed away, Roger called the house asking if your dad could provide him with some documents that he needed to file the taxes for the business. Your dad wasn't doing so well at that time, so Roger directed me to where I could possibly find them. I found what he was looking for in one of the boxes in the closet of the home office. But while searching through the boxes, I came across these files," she says, tapping on the stack of folders. "These files clearly outline that your dad paid for Travis to go to Yale. The letter that appears to come from Yale University announcing the academic scholarship is not from Yale, it's from your dad. I found a draft of the letter that your dad had marked up," she says before clearing her throat.

"Amy, your dad paid for Travis to go to Yale, so that he would be on the other side of the country from you."

I attempt to swallow the lump that's formed in my throat. "But, why? Why would he have done that?"

"You know that your dad wasn't fond of Travis. He thought he was a nice boy, but your dad never wanted you to marry into... well, you know, a middle-class family." I knew that my dad never felt like he had anything in common with Travis' parents, but I never thought he cared so much about it that he felt the need to separate us.

"Why didn't Dad ever express to me that he didn't approve of Travis and his family?"

"You know that your dad never wanted to disappoint you. He never wanted you to know that he didn't accept some of your choices."

I shake my head, feeling betrayed and confused. "Maybe my life would have taken a different turn if

DECEPTION

Travis and I would have gone to college together. Maybe he wouldn't have ended up cheating on me if we hadn't been hundreds of miles apart," I say softly, trying to imagine how my life would have turned out.

"Ames," my mom says, putting a hand on my arm, "Travis never cheated on you."

I furrow my brow. "What do you mean? Travis cheated on me and got Susanna pregnant while we were together."

"No honey, he didn't."

"Yes, he did. Travis has a thirteen-year-old daughter. I spoke with him this week and he told me himself."

"No, Ames. Amanda is not his biological daughter. Amanda is Brian, Travis' brother's daughter. Travis never cheated on you."

I let out an exasperated sigh. "I don't understand any of this."

"Ames, who told you that Travis was cheating on you and that he was the father of Susanna's baby?"

I shrug. "I think it was Dad who first told me. But I recall Susanna's dad, Mr. Lark, talking about it as well."

"Do you know who Mr. Lark was to your dad?"

"I think they were friends," I say, scrunching up my face and shrugging.

"No, they were business partners. Your dad had invested a lot of money in Mr. Lark's construction business. When I found these files, I confronted your dad, and he confessed to me in detail what happened. When Mr. Lark found out that Susanna was pregnant, he agreed to take a sum of money in return for saying that Travis was the father. Your dad knew that was the only way you'd leave Travis."

"But that doesn't make any sense, Mom. How would they get away with something like that?"

"When you have millions of dollars, and as many connections, you can do anything and get away with it."

I'm left speechless. My mom raises her head, looking in the direction of the patio door. I turn around to find Travis standing there with his hands in his pockets. What is he doing at my mom's house?

"Come sit down, you should be here for some of this," she says, motioning for him to sit at the table. He hesitates, looking at me, but then wanders over and pulls a chair out next to her.

I look up at him. "Did you know about all of this? Did your parents know?"

He shakes his head. "I found out when your mom contacted me last spring. My parents knew nothing about it."

DECEPTION

"I called Travis when your dad confessed," my mom intercepts.

"And why did you wait to tell me?" I ask, looking at my mom.

"I knew you would ask that question. And I've been at war with myself over it for the last year. Ames, I didn't want to tell you because I thought that you and Rich had a great relationship. I didn't want to disrupt that."

"So why are you choosing to tell me now?"

"Well, for a couple of reasons," she says, and then pauses, looking afraid to tell me.

"Why?" I demand, wanting her to divulge everything.

"Ames, I'm sick. I'm really sick," she confesses, huffing. I feel the blood rise to my face, my cheeks become flush, and that lump that I was feeling in my throat earlier is back. "I have stage four throat cancer," she adds. Travis places a hand on her arm and lowers his head.

I look at him, briefly taken aback by how comfortable he looks interacting with her. Redirecting my focus back to my mom, I'm unable to speak. "It's terminal. The doctors give me a month to live," she says, with fear radiating in her eyes.

My vision becomes blurry and I feel lightheaded. I try to fight back the tears but they start flowing. I lower my head into my hands and start rocking back and forth.

My mom throws her arms around me, and I lay my head on her shoulder. We both cry together. "It'll be okay, Ames. I promise, it'll be fine," she says in my ear, through sobs. We sit, hugging and crying, for a while.

I finally pull back from her. "Is there more that you need to tell me?" Through a look of defeat, she nods. "What more could there be?" I question, my mouth agape, throwing my hands up in the air.

She leans back in the chair, and I look over at Travis who has barely moved or spoken since he got here.

"While sorting through boxes last week, in an attempt to clean out your dad's office, I found more files that were stashed away in the back of the closet. It appears your dad made an investment in Rich's firm a couple of years back. Has Rich mentioned this to you?"

"No, never."

"Well, he made an investment—which is what they called it anyway. I guess the easiest way to explain it is that it's an investment to ensure that Rich never leaves you."

"What? What's that supposed to mean?"

"This is where things get a bit complicated. I don't understand it all because your dad never mentioned any of this to me. When your dad found out he had cancer, he reached out to Rich to make a contract that included a very large investment in Rich's firm. It came with the agreement that Rich would never leave you in return. I suppose your dad knew that you never wanted to get married to Rich, so he felt that it would be easy for him to leave you, if he ever chose to. I know your dad was fond of the fact that Rich was so successful and wealthy. And I think he wanted to make sure that you were well taken care of after he passed away."

"So, I was a business deal?"

"I truly don't think that your dad saw it that way. I believe he loved you so much that he wanted to make sure you were taken care of, even after he was no longer here to do so himself."

"How do you even know this to be true?" I ask in disbelief.

"I have the contract right here," she replies, tapping on the stack of folders. She pulls out a folder with the word, Europe, written in red marker on the top. I look at her questioningly. "Apparently they referred to this deal as 'Europe.' I don't understand why; I'm sure there's more to it than I've been able to piece together. The parts that I know are in these folders."

"So, Roger must know about all of this?"

"I spoke with Roger after I found these documents and he admitted that he knew about some of them, but he never chose to question your dad for more information. Roger did what he was told to do. You can't pass blame on him."

"Did you know that Rich was—well actually, is cheating on me?" My mom's face becomes expressionless and Travis' mouth drops open.

"Rich?" my mom asks in shock.

"Yeah, he's cheating on me. He's been cheating on me. I caught him with Laura's sister last night. But I found a prepaid cell phone of his that had text messages with another woman from last year as well."

"I had no idea. I thought you guys were happy together. Despite spending a lot of time at work lately, I never thought he would do that to you."

I glance over at Travis, whose expression has changed to anger. He looks down at his lap and shakes his head in disgust.

"Is that why you didn't come on the cruise?" my mom questions.

"No. We didn't go because Rich said he got the time wrong. But I'm convinced he didn't want to go."

DECEPTION

My mom shakes her head. "Did you ever find the letter I gave you?"

"No," I say, narrowing my eyes. "What was in that envelope, anyway?"

"It was a copy of the contract with a note telling you that we need to talk. I couldn't figure out the best way to tell you. I was afraid how you would react. But I knew I had to tell you regardless."

"Why would you choose to give it to me on my birthday?"

"Well, when I invited Rich to your birthday party he immediately declined, saying that he was too busy. Lately he's been distant from us—from you—and he never makes himself available for family gatherings anymore. I asked if he could try to come, and he said he was certain he couldn't, but that he was going to make it up to you by taking you to the island and buying you a car. But what he isn't aware of is that I know he was not the one to pay for your new car or even your day trip to Catalina. These documents, right here, are quite detailed, Amy. You need to look at them. I couldn't allow myself to let this go any longer without you knowing. And with me being sick—" she says, sighing. "I know that I may not have picked the best day to initiate the conversation, but there really is no good day to find out all of this."

We all sit in silence for a while, before my mom gets up from her chair, announcing that she's getting us something to drink. She disappears inside the house.

"And I didn't want to talk about our past with you," I say, smirking. Travis gazes at me and smiles—a beautiful, magnificent smile, without saying a word.

"How are you doing today?" my mom asks Travis when she returns, setting his glass of water on the table and resting her hand on his shoulder.

Not looking up from his hands, he nods. "Not bad."

"How's Amanda doing?"

He covers her hand with his and squeezes it lightly. "Today is one of her good days." So many questions flood my head. I didn't even know that my mom knew about Travis' parents, but it's evident that she does. And she might even know more than that.

"You know about what happened?" I question, looking up at my mom.

"Yes, I know," she says, observing Travis with caring eyes. "It's so tragic, but everything will be all right though."

Travis' phone rings. He answers it while getting up from the chair and walking away from the table. My mom looks at me and smiles. "How are you holding up, honey?"

"I don't know. I'm not sure it's all sunk in yet. I feel like it's too much to even understand."

"I know."

"How are you feeling? Like, how are you really feeling?"

"Well, you know, I'm not too bad," she says, attempting to tell me what I want to hear.

"When did you find out?"

"About three weeks ago. Part of the reason I wanted you, Marla, and Drew to come on vacation was that I wished we could all talk about it together. Marla still doesn't know yet, I left before I could tell her. But Drew knows. I ran into him at the hospital the day that I went in for a biopsy. He's been helping me to understand the test results," she says, her eyes filled with sadness and fear. "It'll be okay though, Ames," she adds, no longer able to look at me. She looks down and starts fidgeting with her dress.

Moving my chair closer to hers, I lean in and hug her. "I love you."

When I pull away, I see that Travis has returned. He places his hands on the back of the chair. "I'll leave you two alone," he says tenderly.

"No, please don't go," my mom declares.

His eyes shift to mine, and I can tell by the look on his face that he really doesn't want to go—and well, I don't want him to go either. "Please stay," I advise, smiling up at him. His eyes instantly brighten and I see a glimmer of a grin form.

"Is Amanda with her grandma?" my mom asks.

"Yeah, she picked Amanda up from school. She's going to sleep over there tonight."

"Then, stay." My mom pulls his chair out. "We can order dinner."

"Amanda isn't your daughter?" I inquire. We've had a couple glasses of wine with dinner and I'm starting to feel more comfortable having Travis in my presence. Although, the alcohol still hasn't helped me to look him in the eye for longer than a few seconds before I start feeling like a schoolgirl with her first crush. If the butterflies in my stomach would go to sleep or flutter away, I'd be good. But at least my inner voice keeps getting louder with every sip of wine, so the butterflies have seemed to settle for a bit.

"She's not my biological daughter, but she's my daughter."

I furrow my brow. "What does that mean?"

"Amanda is Brian's biological daughter. But Brian hasn't been a dad a day in her life. Amanda's mom,

DECEPTION

Susanna, died when she was four. My parents took Amanda in, and then I decided to adopt her when she was ten." I'm left speechless. "She's a remarkable kid," he adds, his smile reaching his eyes.

"She's been through a lot," my mom interjects.

Travis nods. "She has." He notices that I'm not sure what they're talking about, so he elaborates. "Amanda was in a car accident with her mom. They were hit head on by a drunk driver. Their car burst into flames with the impact. Susanna was pronounced dead at the scene, and Amanda was left with third degree burns on seventy-five percent of her body," he explains. "She's had many surgeries and therapies over the last ten years, but she's so resilient and strong. She goes through it all with a smile on her face." I instantly sense the love he has for her, radiating through his words. The feeling of admiration for him invades me.

"What made you adopt her?" I ask, interested in learning more about his love for her.

"Well, my mom was left having to take Amanda to her surgeries and therapies. It was a lot for her to do on her own, so I'd often accompany her. I became drawn to Amanda, and we started creating a bond. Eventually she ended up spending more time with me at work and sleeping over at my house. She even became friends with my neighbors' kids. Eventually, she was more at my house than she was at my parents'. I asked her if she wanted to come live with me," he says, his face lighting up. "And we've been inseparable since. Amanda asked me to be her dad, it was her decision. She's the second-best thing to happen to me." His last statement speaks directly to my heart. It feels like he reached into my chest, took my heart in his hands, and spoke directly to it. I want to ask him what his first best thing is, but I'm afraid to hear his response.

Unsure how to respond, I announce that I need to use the restroom. Getting up with weakened knees, I head inside.

Standing in front of the bathroom mirror, I attempt to give my heart a pep talk. "What are you doing, heart? This is not the time to start acting a fool. Find your composure. You haven't even broken things off with Rich. You don't even know if you want to break things off with Rich. Okay, fine, you do. But you have too much to deal with right now. You can't do this.

"But he's gorgeous. He's so amazingly gorgeous. He adopted his brother's daughter. What man does that? A gorgeous, kind, and selfless one does," the little voice from within interrupts.

Taking long breaths in and out, I convince myself that I need another glass of wine.

DECEPTION

Making my way back outside, I catch my mom and Travis laughing, and I'm stopped dead in my tracks. Watching him laugh sends a chill from the tips of my toes all the way to the top of my head and even down to the tips my fingers. I've missed that laugh.

My mom calls me over and I'm broken from my trance. After I snap out of it, I bustle over to the table. Travis grins slyly at me. Shit, he must have seen me staring at him. After sitting, I take a sip of wine, and it immediately helps to control the fluttering.

"Are you staying at home, Ames?" my mom asks.

"No, I stayed at The Clift last night." I shrug. "I don't know where I'm going to stay while I get my life back together. I just know that I don't want to be at the house another day. It's Rich's house and I don't want to be there."

"Don't stay in a hotel, honey. Come and stay with me. I could use some company, and the house is certainly big enough for the both of us," my mom intercepts.

"I couldn't do that to you. I'll find a place to stay."

"Really, Ames. I could use you here with me. I'd love for you to stay here with me."

I'm quickly reminded about my mom being so sick—that she has only a matter of time left. I swallow hard at the thought and force a smile, nodding. While trying to push the thought out of my mind, I reach for my phone to look at the time and notice that it's still powered off. I turn it on and my phone chimes, listing that I have four voicemails.

"He won't leave me alone. And he got Sarah pregnant," I blurt out before I can even stop the words from forming. Oh, the wine has certainly started to take an effect on me. Damn it, Amy.

"Sarah, Laura's sister?" Travis says, in shock.

"Yeah. Can you believe that?"

"Goodness," my mom responds, shaking her head with disappointment. "I'm so sorry you have to deal with that."

I raise my eyebrows and shrug. "Just think, I was the one to get her a job at his firm a couple of years back."

"I thought he fired her though?" my mom questions.

"I... well, I thought he did too. I don't even know if he did. I don't know if he recently got with her, or what. The text messages that I found from last year were with someone named Olivia, so I don't know," I say, shrugging. Travis and my mom both shake their heads. "But you want to hear something funny?" I say, laughing nervously, "I got a picture of them in the act last night."

DECEPTION

"That would make good marketing material for his business," Travis quips, wide-eyed. We all laugh. I could listen to his laugh all day, all night, and into tomorrow. I can't help but stare at him as he laughs. My phone dings, taking me back to the moment.

I look down to see a text from Laura: *Sorry*

I text back: *We need to talk*

She responds: *I know*

I text: *Tomorrow*

I place the phone down, and take another sip of wine. We spend the next couple hours chatting, catching up, and enjoying the music until my mom announces that she's starting to feel tired and could use some rest.

"I should go anyway," Travis responds, and a sense of disappointment comes over me. Why am I feeling like this?

"You're going to stay here tonight, right?" my mom pleads.

"Sure. I do need to go get my things from the hotel though."

"Okay. I'll get you the spare key, in case I'm in bed when you return." My mom stands from her chair and starts clearing the table.

"Go inside, I can take care of this," I advise, taking the glasses out of her hands.

"Yeah, Mom, go get your rest," Travis says. Did he call her mom? I'm frozen for a minute, trying to let the words sink in, making sure I heard correctly. I did hear correctly.

He grabs some of the dishes that remain on the table, and our arms briefly brush as he passes me on his way into the kitchen. It's like a shock of electricity surges through my body, and my breath hiccups.

We clear the remaining dishes in silence, and stack them in the sink. Travis turns the water on. "No, Travis, don't do that. I can wash them," I say, shaking my head.

"I can help you," he responds, turning the water back off.

"I can do it when I get back. I don't think I'll be sleeping much tonight anyway. It appears that I have a lot of reading to catch up on," I say, motioning to the stack of files. He nods hesitantly.

We stand a moment longer, gazing at each other. Come on, lungs, wake up. He looks away. "Okay, well I'm going to get going."

"Yeah. I have to go get my things at the hotel so I'll walk out with you."

Walking outside, it's gotten dark and the lights from the porch illuminate the path to the driveway. We stand by my car, and it feels like he doesn't want to walk away. My heart doesn't either. Come on, heart, we can do this.

"So, I'll call you on Monday so we can meet again to finish up the details about the case?"

He shuffles from one foot to the other and shoves his hands in his pockets. "Well, we won't need to meet about the case anymore. My brother confessed today."

"What?"

"The detective called me on my way here to tell me that Brian confessed to killing them both. He admitted that he acted alone, so I'm no longer a suspect."

"Why? I mean, why would he have killed his own parents?"

"Meth. Drugs have turned Brian into someone other than my brother over the years," he says with disappointment in his voice. "I know he's my brother, but he's better off behind bars," he adds, his head lowered.

"I'm so sorry, Travis," I say, not really knowing how else to respond.

He raises his head and shrugs. "Thanks."

"All right. Well, I guess… good night." I'm no longer able to look at him so sad—and well, so sexy—much longer before I start to melt into the driveway.

"Will you be okay?" he asks, with concern in his eyes. I nod and offer a smile. "Good night, Amy." He hesitates and then turns in the direction of his car.

I pick my heart up off the ground, and it rides shotgun all the way to the hotel.

chapter nine

Monday
April 22, 2013
8:23 a.m.

    I spent the weekend looking over the papers my mom gave me. I had her answer some questions that she was able to, but there is still so much that is left unknown. I have to realize that some of it may always remain a mystery. The one thing I wish I could understand is why my dad felt the need to do that to me, or for me, like my mom claims. He almost lost his daughter when I attempted suicide over it, and he made me stay with a man for seven years who evidently didn't really love me. For what? Because I was the one child of his that decided to follow in his footsteps and study law? Or, because I was his baby girl that he always wanted to protect? None of it makes sense to me, and I'm having a hard time coming to terms with it. My mom told me how close she's gotten with Travis over the last year. He's been visiting her a lot since she told him about the truth, even bringing Amanda by to see her. She glows when she speaks about him. It's evident that she adores him; it's like she's speaking about one of her own children. She also admitted that she knew he was the one leaving me the sunflowers. She said that he talks about me often. I can't hold back the smile when I think about that.

I also spoke with Laura on Saturday, and she confessed that she knew about her sister and Rich, but she only found out last Friday when her sister was in hysterics, telling her that she was pregnant. Sarah says that it wasn't planned and Rich was angry when she told him. He tried convincing her to get an abortion, claiming that it would ruin him. Laura said that she called Rich on Saturday morning, demanding that he tell me about the affair, but he told her that he didn't care what she wanted. He said that he wasn't going to tell me anything because it was going to ruin his career. And then he hung up on her. As soon as she told me, the phone call that I overheard on Saturday made sense;

it was Laura he was speaking to. Laura was confused as to why he would claim it would ruin his career until I told her about everything that my mom uncovered. She's angry with her sister, feeling like she not only betrayed me but also Laura since we've been best friends our whole lives. I've had a lot of time to think and try to process everything this weekend. I'm certain that I need to get out of the house, I need to move on. The funny thing is that all the anger I felt days ago has seemed to subside. I want to focus my attention on my mom since the time we've spent together this weekend has confirmed that she's very sick. I'm so grateful that she had the strength to tell me about it all. She needs me right now, and she doesn't need a broken me, so I'm going to be strong not only for me but for her.

I'm driving to the house to get the things that I'll need for now, and I'll return later to get the rest. But there's not much in the house that is solely mine. I know that Rich won't be there since he leaves for work so early in the morning.

On my way, I phone Julie at the office. "Good morning, Julie. Can you let Matthew know that the Littletons will be in today? Tell him that I won't be there, but he has all the information he needs to meet with them by himself. I don't have anything else on my schedule today, do I?"

"No, that was all you had. Is everything all right, Amy?"

"Yes. I'm moving today."

"Oh."

I pull into the driveway and I'm shocked his car is here. Damn it! What is he still doing home? I put the car in reverse and back out. I'll have to return later. Seconds later, my phone dings.

It's a text message from Rich: *I saw you pull up. Can we please talk?*

Shit! He must have been waiting for me, knowing that I'd go by while he was at work. I contemplate driving and not responding, but I really want to get this over with. I circle around the neighborhood and drive back to the house. Rich is sitting on the stairs when I pull into the driveway. I take a deep breath and get out of the car. "You can do this, Amy. Go in and get your things," my inner voice confidently advises.

I walk up the pathway and ascend the front stairs. "I'm here to get my things," I say, walking past him, looking away.

"Can we please talk first? I need to explain."

"I don't care to listen to you, Rich. I've made up my mind."

DECEPTION

He tugs my arm in his direction. "Please, Amy. I know you don't want to stay, but I need to explain myself."

"Explain what? I don't care to listen to you try to justify your actions," I respond, pulling my arm out of his hand, feeling disgusted that he touched me.

"Amy, give me a few minutes. I promise to let you do what you want afterward."

I take in an exasperated breath. "Fine. Talk."

"Can you sit down? Come on, Amy."

I slump down on the stairs below him, looking away and not saying a word.

"When we met I instantly fell in love with you."

I roll my eyes. "I don't—" I attempt to say before he cuts me off.

"Please, hear me out," he says with desperation in his voice. "I fell in love with you. I thought what we had was going to last a lifetime. You are strong-willed, determined, and so smart. I fell in love with it all. Over the years, our careers became more demanding but we worked hard at making our relationship work. I feel like we did a pretty good job at it. It wasn't until about two years ago that your dad approached me with an investment plan. He wanted to make a substantial investment in my company. It sounded great until he presented me with some stipulations. He wanted to invest in my company so that I could expand into the European market; he claimed to have connections there. One of the conditions stated that I could never leave you or I'd lose it all. At first, it was all confusing and I couldn't see myself agreeing to it. I was surprised that he was even suggesting it. But then, I got to thinking that I was going to be with you forever anyway so what harm would there be in it. It took a while, but I finally agreed to it and he even had me sign a contract. He connected me with some businessmen in Europe, and things started to develop and grow. I tried to put the thought of the contract behind me, but instead I started to lose respect for your dad. I couldn't look at him the same way as I once did. And I started feeling guilty for agreeing to this deal behind your back. Subconsciously, I began distancing myself from you. I wanted to tell you about it, but your dad was sick and I knew you didn't have much longer with him. I couldn't get myself to tell you that your dad had proposed all that right before he died. That seemed too cruel." He huffs before hesitating.

"The more time I started spending at work, it drew me to Olivia. I didn't mean for it to happen. On Valentine's Day I was out with Olivia at Alexander's and your dad happened to show up to pick up dinner. He saw me with Olivia and he demanded that I tell you about it, or that I leave you and he would break all the connections I had in Europe as result." He shakes his head with an expression of shame on his face. "I broke up with Olivia. I even fired her because I couldn't stand seeing her every day, while not being able to be with her. I couldn't see my business losing all of that. I'm not proud of it, Amy. I got so wrapped up in the success that the connections in Europe brought to my company."

I remain quiet, looking down at my hands. I also remain emotionless. If he's looking for someone to feel bad for him, he better look elsewhere.

"After your dad died, Olivia started texting me more and more. I agreed to see her, and things started back up. I'm not trying to make excuses, but I fell in love with her."

My heart takes a nosedive straight down to my toes. Did he say he loves Olivia? Wasn't he just with Sarah? He's a bigger scum than I thought he could ever be.

Unable to hold back any longer, I look him square in the eyes. "So let me get this straight, you have a serious relationship for seven years with me, you claim to love Olivia, but you're screwing Sarah?"

"Olivia is Sarah," he says. "Her name is Sarah Olivia Watson. I call her Olivia."

I clench my teeth. "I don't think I want to hear anything more, Rich," I say, pushing myself up from the stairs. "I'm going to get my things and I'll be on my way."

"I've already moved my stuff out."

"Why are you moving out? This is your house, you paid for it. I'm certainly not going to stay."

"This house isn't mine. Your dad bought this house for us—well, really, for you."

"I thought you bought this house?" I question, confused.

"No. This house was part of the deal. This house, that car—" he says waving in the direction of my new Lamborghini. "All of it is from your dad," he adds, before pressing his lips together and nodding slightly while lowering his head. "Now that you're leaving me, I'm left with nothing. Everything, including my business, goes to you. Your dad's buddy, Joseph, has the contract with all the details."

Whoa. That's a lot to swallow. None of the papers I read over mentioned that the house or his company would be mine if he were to ever leave me.

I push open the front door and Rich stands, turning around in my direction. "I'm really sorry, Amy. I never wanted to hurt you. Having too much fortune has ruined me. I'm so sorry."

DECEPTION

I raise my eyebrows, tighten my lips, and shrug. Then I turn and close the door behind me.

While walking around the house, the words that Rich spoke replay in my head. All of the furniture is still here and everything is still in its place, just as I left it on Thursday. Looking into the office, I notice Rich's desk is completely bare. I walk upstairs and our bedroom appears to be untouched, except that the TracFone is no longer on Rich's pillow. I open the door to Rich's closet to find it empty. Leaning against the door jamb, I gaze in, remaining without emotion. I'm completely out of feeling for what happened, for everything that Rich told me, for the fact that my live-in boyfriend of seven years has left, and for the thought that my dad initiated all of it. What am I to do now? This house is mine, but it doesn't feel like home right now.

I snatch a few suitcases from the hallway closet. Regardless of what I choose to do, I'm going to stay with my mom for now. She needs me and, frankly, I need her. I return to the bedroom and lay the suitcases on the bed. The house feels so quiet—so somber. I place my iPhone into the docking station and play some music. I turn it up loud, attempting to drown out the silence, and I start packing clothes from my drawers into the suitcases.

I walk to my closet and remove suits and dresses from the hangers. When I bend down to grab a few pairs of shoes, I see a large box stashed on the floor in the back of my closet. Remembering what I have in the box, I pull it out and sit cross-legged on the floor.

I open it up and start taking out the photo albums, yearbooks, and scrapbooks. While looking through the albums, memories of high school flood me and times with Travis consume me. Tears form and fall from my eyes with every page that I turn. This was the time of my life that I was most happy, and these pictures prove it. Photos of me and my friends acting silly, of me and Travis on our hiking trips, of me and my family at my birthday parties, and of me and Travis at our prom. In every picture, I was so happy—we were so happy.

I reach into the bottom of the box and take out a shoebox. Not remembering what's inside, I open it and I'm taken aback. Inside the box lies dried up sunflowers. How could I not have thought that the sunflowers placed on my car could have been from Travis? He knew they were my favorite, so he'd given me sunflowers often.

DECEPTION

My hands start shaking and my chest feels tight. Bending my legs to my chest and hugging them, I lay my head on my knees and cry. I cry for what I once had, for how happy I once was, and because it was all torn away from me without my own doing.

I'm startled when I feel a hand on my arm. Looking up, I see Travis bent down next to me. His eyes are glazed over with tears. Hesitantly, he kneels on the floor and wraps his arms around me. I don't pull back. Instead, I rest my head on his shoulder and we both cry. Realizing that he needs consoling as much I do, I remove my arms from around my legs and reach around his shoulders, pulling him closer. I let out a heavy sigh of relief. It feels good to be in his arms. I've missed this—so-much-so that I try to think about how I could have gone so long without it. He smells sweet, his arms around me feel amazing, and the sound of his breathing helps to calm me. We remain in this position long after we both have stopped crying.

Eventually, I pull my head off of his shoulder. "Hi," I acknowledge.

"Hi."

"Sorry for slobbering all over your shirt."

He smiles. "It's okay, I was going to throw out this old thing anyway," he says with a hint of sarcasm.

"How did you even know I was here?"

"Your mom told me that you were here moving your things out. I thought maybe you could use some help."

"Thanks."

He pulls away from me and sits back, leaning up against the wall of the closet across from me. I'm left feeling sad—not because he's here, or for the uncertainty of my future, but that he pulled away. He stretches out his legs and looks around the closet.

Without hesitation, I ask him the one question that I've wanted to know for the past thirteen years. "Why didn't you try to contact me after I broke up with you?"

"What do you mean? I did. I called you, but you never answered. Then you went and blocked my calls so I couldn't anymore."

"You called twice, on the same day that I broke up with you. And I never answered because I was still so angry with you. But I never blocked your calls. A part of me wanted you to contact me. I would've never blocked your number."

"Well, when I called your cell phone the day after you broke up with me, I got a message that said that my number was blocked. I even tried calling your apartment phone and my number was blocked from that too." I shake my head, confused. "When I realized that I couldn't get in touch with you on the phone, I tried to

DECEPTION

figure out a way to get money for a plane ticket to come to California, but I didn't have that kind of money. I wanted to come and see you so badly, but I couldn't. So, I decided to write you letters. I wrote you a lot. You can't overlook those."

"What letters?" I ask, perplexed.

"Are you kidding? I wrote you a dozen or so letters. The first one that I mailed to the college was returned to me undeliverable. I later found out that you had dropped out for the semester and returned home, so I sent the letters there instead. Please don't tell me that you forgot about those letters."

"Travis, I swear I never got a single letter from you. I promise," I say, surprised by what I'm hearing. He raises his eyebrows and shakes his head in disbelief. "Have you had a good life?"

He shrugs. "It hasn't been bad. I've had my fair share of ups and downs." I nod.

He stands and, bending down, he extends a hand. I look up at him. He motions for me to grab it. I do. He leads me into the bedroom and, while still clasping my hand, he pulls his hand up to his chest. He reaches behind my waist with his other hand and pulls me in. "Dance with me," he says tenderly, holding his gaze on mine. I wrap my arms around his shoulders and rest my cheek against his, and we dance.

When the song is over, I remove my cheek from his. "No, please, let's dance," he whispers. So, we do.

We dance right through the next four songs, and after there are no more songs playing. We move slowly, while holding each other close, dancing to the beat of our hearts.

He plants a kiss in my hair, and I snuggle in a bit more.

"I've missed you," I confess. I can feel him nod.

"I've missed you so much, Sweets."

I pull my head back and look at him. My heart starts dancing, and a smile forms on both of our faces. Travis always called me Sweets, which was his pet name for me. "You remembered."

"How could I forget?" he responds, and then pauses. "Do you trust me?"

I stifle a laugh. "Well, after the events from the past couple of weeks, I'm left unsure of who I can trust anymore."

He tilts his head, looking at me. "But do you trust me?" I smile and nod. "There's something I want to show you," he says, lowering his hand from my waist. I look at him with questioning eyes.

"I can only imagine what he can show me," my inner voice shouts. I smile and suppress a laugh.

"What?"

DECEPTION

I shake my head, realizing that I was caught laughing by myself. "Nothing. What do you want to show me?" I ask, trying to redirect his attention.

"Come with me." He takes me by the hand, and we walk out of the bedroom and down the stairs. He opens up the front door, leading me outside. The moment my feet step onto the porch, something catches my eye. My jaw drops open.

"You still have it?"

He nods.

Sitting in the middle of my driveway is Travis' 1972 Cadillac Convertible that I once loved so much. Travis and his dad would spend hours in the garage restoring it. And it still looks exactly as it did back in high school.

I scurry down the stairs and over to it, barely feeling my legs under me. Everything is exactly as I remember it, and it even still smells like it once did.

"Want a ride?"

"Yes," I exclaim. "Give me a minute."

Running back inside the house, I grab my phone from the bedroom. Then, I get my keys and lock the front door behind me. He stands with the passenger door open, waiting for me. He looks so good next to this car, and memories of us immediately overtake me.

Sitting down, I feel the stitched leather seat, I run my fingers on the dashboard, and I lay my head back on the headrest while Travis gets in behind the wheel. He turns the key in the ignition and the car comes to life.

"This is so exciting," I announce, giddy. He smiles.

Turning up the music, we drive through the neighborhood and the city. We get onto the highway and drive. I find myself lost in the moment, in the music, and in time. He pulls up, turning the engine off. Suddenly, everything looks familiar.

I look over at him. "What are we doing here?"

He doesn't say anything, he simply smiles.

He gets out, and then walks over to my side, opening my door. Reaching out his hand for me, I hesitate, but then take it in mine. I get out and he leads me to the front door of the Love Shack. When we walk in, it looks as if as the place is empty until someone appears from the kitchen.

"Good morning, Mr. Cashman," the gentleman says.

"They know you by name here?" I whisper.

"They better," Travis says. "I'm their boss." Someone bring me the paddles because it feels like my heart just went into cardiac arrest... again.

"What?" I question, in shock.

"This place is mine. I own it," he says, with a glimmer of a grin.

"Do you realize that I recently found this place? I love this place." He nods but doesn't say anything. "Travis, really, I'm not kidding. I love this place. I was here three times in one week after I discovered it."

He cocks an eyebrow and takes my hand, leading me to the patio. He pulls out a chair at the table, and motions for me to sit. He sits across from me, still not letting go of my hand. "You sat right there."

"What?"

"The time I saw you here, you were sitting right in that chair."

Surprised by his words, I cover my mouth with my hand. "You saw me here?"

His eyes light up. "You were here with someone—a friend, I'm assuming. It was the same day that you kicked me out of your office. I drove back here after you gave me the boot," he says, with a sly grin. "It wasn't an hour later that I hear Lisa Ann ask the bartender for a red raspberry martini with Chambord. I immediately came out from the kitchen. We don't get that request often, and I've always remembered that was how you drank your martinis. Every time someone orders it, I always look to see who it is, hoping that it might be you, but it never was, until last Tuesday when

I saw you sitting here. It felt surreal to me. I've always wanted to see you here, but never thought I would."

The bartender comes over. "With Chambord, ma'am," he says, setting a red raspberry martini in front of me. He then places a beer in front of Travis.

"Can I buy you a drink?" Travis asks, smiling at me. The butterflies return, and they flutter harder than ever.

"I thought you went to college for engineering?" I ask, trying to redirect my attention and calm the fluttering.

"Hmm, yeah I did. But I only stayed at Yale through two weeks of the second semester of my freshman year. I was flunking out of my classes because, well, I wasn't going to class. After you broke up with me, I spent the entire day in bed and the night partying. I stopped caring about what I was there for. I decided that I didn't want to be there anymore. Because I didn't care to find a job, I didn't have any money, so the nights of partying stopped and I lost interest in everything. My parents got some money to pay for a plane ticket and I returned home. I helped my dad out in his shop for a while, but that didn't provide me with much money so I decided to get a job tending bar. I started to enjoy it—I liked the nightlife and the people. I started to save up to move out of my parents' house. I ended up getting my own place a few months later. Then, I decided that I wanted to save up to get my own bar. I came across this place five years ago. It was vacant, but I fell in love with it instantly. I decided to buy it right away, outright. Over the years, I invested more and more into it, renovating it. I think I'm satisfied with how it is right now," he says, nodding and looking around.

"That's so remarkable, Travis," I say, squeezing his hand that's still clasping mine.

He raises my hand to his mouth and kisses it gently. "Thanks." I feel like someone turned up the heat. I become flush and melt in my chair.

He stands, tugging on my hand. "Come with me."

Walking in front of me, he leads me inside. He stops in front of a wall filled with pictures. Unclasping our hands, he stretches his arm around my shoulder. With his other hand, he points to a picture directly in the center of all the others.

I gasp and put my hand over my mouth. I stare directly at a picture of me and Travis sitting on a rock, and kissing. It's from one of our hiking trips. I remember the moment well. We took that picture right after he gave me my promise ring. "That's us."

"Yeah. That used to be my favorite memory."

I look up at the words above the pictures that read: *Soul Mates*.

A tear runs down my cheek. While I rest my head on his shoulder, his last words sink in.

I raise my head and look at him. "It used to be your favorite memory, but it's not anymore?"

"I now have a new favorite; this here, right now."

I try to catch my breath, while more tears form. He squeezes my arm and pulls me closer. "I'm really going to have to trash this shirt now," he quips, and then kisses my forehead.

chapter ten

Wednesday
April 24, 2013
10:23 a.m.

"All right, Amy. I think we got all the grays covered," Tracy says, wrapping the foil around the last strands of hair. "Now it's time to sit under the dryer for a bit."

Going over to the dryer, I sit. While scrolling through my work email on my phone, it dings with a new text message. When I see it's from Travis, I begin to feel giddy.

Travis: *Hi*

I close my eyes and imagine his voice. We spent yesterday texting back and forth. It appears the awkwardness that we felt the first couple of times seeing each other has subsided because we can't seem to get enough of each other. I haven't felt like this in so long. It feels good.

Me: *Hi*

Travis: *What are you doing?*

Me: *At the salon, getting my natural highlights colored.*

Travis: *Why would you color them? Gray highlights are hot!*

My eyes widen, sensing that he's flirting: *Why couldn't you have told me that before I got my head covered in foil?* ☺

Travis: *It's okay. It has to grow out eventually.* ☺

I'm completely flush, and it has absolutely nothing to do with the fact I'm sitting under a hot hairdryer.

Travis: *What time is your mom's appointment?*

Me: *It's at 11:30. I'm nervous.*

My mom has a doctor's appointment, and the doctor requested that her kids accompany her. He has some things he'd like to go over with us. I'm nervous and scared to hear what he has to say. Over the past couple days, her voice has become hoarser and she's been coughing a lot. I'm trying hard to be strong for her, but it's difficult to see her go through this.

Travis: *Everything will be fine. Can you text me when you get out of the appointment?*

Me: *I hope you're right. Sure, I'll text you. Are you at work today?*

Travis: *Yeah. Here until 1:30. Then I'm picking Amanda up from school.*

Tracy comes over to check on my hair. "You look like you're up to something," she says when she sees me grinning from ear to ear.

"No," I say, shaking my head and trying to hide my smile.

"Are you talking to Travis?"

"Maybe," I say, biting down on my lower lip.

"Keep that smile on you, girl, I like it," she says, walking away.

Me, to Travis: *Can I confess something to you?*

Travis: *Now I'm the one that's nervous.*

Me: *So, you don't want to hear what I have to say?*

Travis: *Ah, okay, give it to me.*

I type out: *I know that I went thirteen years without seeing you, and I saw you two days ago, but am I completely crazy if I miss you already?*

My finger hovers over the Send button, unsure if I'm crossing a line that I probably shouldn't. I might end up scaring him away, but I can't help it. I haven't been able to focus at all since I left him on Monday. Before I convince myself to press Send, another text comes through.

Travis: *Did you want to confess that you don't want to talk to me anymore? Because you sure are silent right now.*

I press Send and close my eyes. "Please don't take it the wrong way. Please don't get scared," I mutter under my breath. It feels like a lifetime goes by before my phone dings.

Travis: *Sorry, it took me a while to catch up to my heart. It jumped out of my chest and started sprinting to San Fran. I miss you so much, Sweets.*

I let out a huge sigh of relief, pressing the phone against my chest, letting all of his words speak directly to my heart.

Tracy comes over again. "Sorry but your sexting time is over," she announces. I pout and text Travis.

Me: *Sorry, I have to go. Tracy is pulling me back into reality. Gotta go check out my new hair and then head to the doctor. Text you later?*

Travis: *I'll be waiting.*

"You're bitten by the love bug," Tracy says, pushing me on the shoulder teasingly.

I scrunch up my face and close my eyes. "I know."

"I sure love it."

I pick my mom up at her house and we drive to the doctor's office. She appears as nervous as I am. My brother and sister are both there waiting for us. After sitting a bit in the waiting room, we're lead into Dr. Bridestone's office. He explains that my mom's cancer is terminal because it's spread to other organs and her bones throughout her body, and it's spreading quite fast. He says that she will soon need around the clock care, and he suggests that she consider checking into a facility if it's not possible to get her a nurse at home. The expression on my mom's face tells me that she doesn't want to go to a facility, and I know she wants to be at home.

"My mom has dedicated her life to taking care of her family. There is no way that she will be placed in a facility. We will get her the care that she needs," I chime in, knowing that my brother and sister both agree. We spoke about it yesterday and we decided that she will stay at home.

My mom squeezes my hand and mouths, "thank you," through tear-stained eyes.

Dr. Bridestone stresses that she will always need someone by her side, even at night, because if she should start coughing, she may need assistance. I feel numb listening to him speak so casually about it while she sits there. I know he does this countless times, but I don't, and it's my mom he's speaking of.

We walk out of the doctor's office and I'm choking back tears. "That was hard," I state to my brother, while my mom walks ahead, holding onto my sister's arm.

"It was. I deal with this stuff every day as a doctor, but it certainly never feels like this," he responds, putting his arm around me and squeezing.

"She's gotten worse over the past couple of days."

"I can tell by seeing how she looks today," he remarks, shaking his head in sadness. "Damn, cancer."

We get her back home and up to her bedroom to rest. Drew, Marla, and I sit in the living room and we make a plan that one of us will be with her at all times. "I bet Aunt Jackie would want to help too. I'll call her today," Marla says. Aunt Jackie is my mom's only sister and they're really close.

My phone rings. I look down to see that it's Julie. "Hi Julie."

"Hi Amy. I'm sorry to bother you. I know that you're busy, but there's a gentleman by the name of Joseph Greenbach who called here. He said that he needs to meet with you sometime today. Something about a contract? Do you want me to ask what exactly it is that he needs?"

"Joseph Greenbach?"

"Yeah. He said he's an attorney."

Immediately I recall who Mr. Greenbach is. He's my father's attorney friend, who drew up the contract between my dad and Rich. "Oh, yes, I know who he is. Did he say what time he could meet?"

"He said any time after one o'clock."

"I really don't want to do this today, but fine. Schedule him in for two-thirty," I say, feeling disgusted for even having to deal with this.

"Amy, you've been with Mom so much the past few days, you need a break. I'll stay with her today. You get some work done and get a good night's rest," Marla advises when I get off the phone.

"Are you sure?"

"Don't even think twice, Amy. Mom is lucky to have you here with her. I know you have work to get done, and you haven't slept in days. I will stay with her tonight."

"Thank you."

Before leaving, my brother agrees to come by tomorrow to stay with our mom for the day. And I'll stay with her overnight.

I text Travis when I get to work.

Me: *Appointment went as well as it could. She's home resting. The doctor recommends someone be with her at all times so my brother, sister and I are taking shifts.*

My phone rings seconds after I press Send. It's Travis calling. "Hi."

There's a brief pause before he responds. "Hi. Sorry it took me a bit to respond, I was trying to catch my breath."

"What are you doing that you need to catch your breath?"

"Nothing. I'm listening to your voice."

Yup, he did it to me again. I'm completely melting in my chair.

"Have you been listening to my thoughts?" I shoot back. He doesn't say anything but I can feel him smiling through the phone.

"So, how's Mom doing?" he asks.

"Considering the situation, she's okay I guess."

"So, do you guys need more help? You know, do you need someone to stay with her sometimes?"

"Well, there's Marla, Drew, and myself who will stay in shifts. And I think my Aunt Jackie will help as well."

DECEPTION

"I'll take a few shifts," he quickly interjects, kindness overflowing from every word.

"Oh, Travis, you don't have to."

"But what if I want to?"

"Really?"

"Yeah, I really do."

"Okay, I'll let Marla know. She's the one putting the schedule together."

"Good. So do you have to stay with your mom tonight?"

"No, Marla is there tonight."

"Well, Amanda is staying at a friend's house tonight since they don't have school tomorrow. Can I possibly cook you dinner?"

"Yes," I respond even before he can finish.

"Well, okay then," he quips, sounding amused.

"Your place? What time?"

"Yes, and how about six o'clock? And this is an official date, so don't be late. Actually, the host recommends that you arrive early—like, hours early." I close my eyes, and soak in his voice and those words.

"I'll be there at four o'clock then. I suppose I need your address too."

"127 Oakwood Avenue."

Julie knocks on the door. "Mr. Greenbach is here."

"I'm sorry, but my appointment that I'm dreading is here," I say into the phone.

"Is everything all right?"

"It will be. I just need to get through this."

After hanging up and taking a moment to come down from my natural high, I invite Mr. Greenbach in. He starts by introducing himself. And then he presents me with the contract, which details that Rich is signing over his company to me. He states that I simply need to sign a few papers to make the agreement official.

I push the contract away. "I won't be signing anything," I say firmly. He looks at me questionably. "Mr. Greenbach, I respect you as an attorney, but I certainly don't respect you for helping my dad to create this contract and agreeing to act in his absence."

I take the contract and tear it in half, and then tear it in half once more. And I continue to tear it until all that is left is a pile of tiny pieces of paper in the middle of the table.

"If I were to agree to this contract that I never even knew about, let alone had any part of creating, it would make me as shameful as those who created it and agreed to it. I refuse to be a monster. You can tell Rich that I will not be taking over his company, it's his to keep," I advise, standing up. "Now you can see yourself out."

DECEPTION

I check my watch and see that it's three-ten, so I gather my things and tell Julie that I will see her tomorrow. Fifty minutes later, I'm pulling into 127 Oakwood Avenue. I adjust my dress and check my lipstick in the rear-view mirror, and then I stroll up to the front door.

Travis greets me, opening the door even before I reach the top stairs. He stands in the doorway, looking at me while holding out a sunflower.

"Thank you, sir," I say playfully. Reaching for it, I notice that it has a tag attached to it that reads: *Hi*.

"Hi," I say, looking into his eyes and reaching out for his other hand.

He pulls me in for a hug. "I'm so happy you're here. Nice hair, by the way." He leads me into the house and gives me a guided tour, pausing in the kitchen to hand me a glass of wine.

We continue walking around the house. It's a cute, quaint home, but I can't help but notice how clean it is.

"Are you sure you don't have a woman living here?" I remark, standing in the upstairs hallway outside of his bedroom.

He looks around and furrows his brow. "No, it's just me and Amanda. Why do you ask that?"

"This place is immaculate. I'm really impressed."

"Thanks. But I can't take all the credit, Amanda and I make a good team," he responds, grinning.

His remark makes me smile. "I love how your face lights up when you talk about her."

"I can't wait for you to meet her. You'll instantly know why I love her so much," he says with conviction in his words. He has no idea what his love for her does to me.

I shake my head and smile. "Yup, you're amazing."

He wraps his hands around my waist. "You are amazing, Sweets." Chills run up and down my body while I breathe him in.

I can't help myself, I kiss him lightly on the neck, and he takes in a sharp breath. I close my eyes and pull him closer. We stand in the hallway without speaking. Minutes go by until he exhales and shakes his head.

I lean back enough to look at him. "What's the matter?"

"Absolutely nothing. Ab—sol—ute—ly not a thing. It feels so good to finally have you in my arms again. I've waited my entire life for this moment."

I smile and plant a kiss on his cheek.

He pauses, looking contemplatively, and then grabs my hand and leads me back downstairs. Part of me—a very small part of me—is thankful he did because his bedroom was looking more and more appealing by the minute.

"I hope you still like lobster," he states once we reach the kitchen.

"Are you serious? We're having lobster?" I ask with excitement.

"We're having Surf and Turf for the main course, and a surprise for dessert." He grins.

"I haven't had lobster in so long. I'm excited we're having lobster."

He laughs. "So, I guess that means that you still like it then?"

I nod with wide eyes.

During dinner, I tell him about my visit with Attorney Greenbach. "I admire you for not agreeing to it. You have no idea how much I respect you for being the bigger person and taking the higher ground in all of that mess." He takes my hand and looks at me attentively with those eyes—those beautiful gray eyes that peer directly into my soul. I have to look away.

"I thought I'd be taking it much harder than I actually am. I can't explain why I haven't completely lost it. But I guess that I've cried enough over someone who evidently didn't even love me. I refuse to shed another tear for him. I'm still trying to figure out how I feel about my dad though."

"I've spent a lot of time over the last year being downright angry with your dad. But your mom helped me to see past all the hate and realize that if two people are meant to be together, they'll find a way. I guess this is our test," he says, winking.

"I think we've already passed." I squeeze his hand.

While clearing the table, Travis asks if I want dessert. He then takes a red velvet cake out of the refrigerator. "I know I'm twelve days late, but I haven't been able to celebrate your birthday for thirteen years, so I figure being late by only twelve days is excusable."

"You know, you're as sweet today as you were thirteen years ago," I say, walking over to him and putting my hands around him.

"I feel like the luckiest man in the world right now," he responds, hugging me close and kissing my forehead.

I rest my head on his shoulder. "Luck has nothing to do with this, it's all fate," I whisper.

He pulls away and I'm taken aback. He bites down on his lower lip. I look at him from the corner of my eye questioningly. "I hope you don't think that I'm moving too fast, but I've waited far too long for this moment, and I feel like the years apart have just been a pause—albeit, a long pause. I found something the other day that I think you should have."

He reaches into his pocket and takes my hand, opening my palm face up. He lays something in it, and my jaw drops open.

"My promise ring," I say, gasping in shock. "Where did you find it?"

"It was at your mom's house. She kept it," he responds, looking nervous and unsure.

I slide it on my finger and it fits as perfectly as it did when I was eighteen. Putting my hand up to my chest, I press it, hugging it with my other hand. Feeling a tear form, I reach out for him and wrap my arms around his shoulders. "I will never take it off again," I whisper.

He pulls me in tight, wrapping his arms around my waist and I kiss his neck through tears. I pull my head away and we stand there gazing at each other. I want to kiss him so badly that my entire body aches with desire.

I can't hold back any longer. I place my hands on the sides of his face, and I plant a gentle kiss on his lips. I hear him inhale. He pulls me in, resting his hand on the back my head. He kisses me like I haven't been kissed in quite some time, and it's like I have my own personal fireworks show coursing through my body. I run my fingers through his hair. The touch of his lips to mine consumes me. His lips part and I feel the warmth of his tongue search mine. I get lost in his passion while his gentleness brings me back to days past.

Placing his hands on the sides of my face, he looks into my eyes and then kisses the corner of my mouth, my nose, my eyes, my forehead, my cheeks, my chin, my jaw, and my neck. I feel my knees weaken under me.

"Goodness, how I've missed kissing you," he whispers.

"I've missed you," I respond, and then close my eyes, trying to find equanimity.

"I really think we should have some cake now," he remarks, distracting us from the raw desire that we're both experiencing.

We eat cake and decide to watch a movie. I lay on the couch wrapped in his arms, and there is no place I'd rather be. He gently brushes his fingers through my hair. It must have put me to sleep because I wake up when I feel him kissing my cheek, but I don't open my eyes, I enjoy the moment. He kisses me again, and I pull my head back, exposing my neck. He chuckles when he notices that I'm awake.

"Stay with me tonight?"

I open my eyes. "I wish I could, but I have to be at work early tomorrow to prepare for trial next week."

He pouts. "I understand." He kisses the corner of my mouth. His tender kiss electrifies me.

"I really need to go before I change my mind."

We stroll, arm-in-arm, slowly to my car, and I can sense that he doesn't want me to go. And every single part of me doesn't either. "I hope you don't have plans for Saturday," he says, grabbing hold of me and pulling me close to him. I look at him inquisitively. "I planned a spa day for you and your mom, as a belated birthday gift."

"Travis, thank you," I say endearingly.

"I figured that you both could use the pampering."

"You are the most wonderful man ever. Thank you," I say before pulling him in and losing myself in the taste of his mouth. "I have to go. I really have to go. Like right now," I add, shaking my head and peeling myself away from him. He takes my hand in his, pulling it up to his mouth, and kisses my ring.

"Can you text me when you get home so I know you made it there safe?"

"I will."

Clasping his hands behind his head, he watches me get in the car and hesitantly pull out of the driveway.

chapter eleven

Saturday
April 27, 2013
9:11 a.m.

My mom and I lay side-by-side on our stomachs, enjoying our massage. She's having a pretty good day and is in good spirits. But she's also been coughing more the past couple of days, and her voice has become more of a whisper.

"This feels nice."

"It does. Travis is really sweet to do this for us."

"He is," I respond, my heart content.

"So, how are things going with you two? You seem to be getting along quite nicely," she says, smiling.

DECEPTION

"It's so nice to have him back in my life. Sometimes it feels like we were never apart. He's still the same sweet guy I remember. I can't help but wonder how I could have gone so long without him. Having him around has helped me get through everything that I've had to deal with the past couple weeks."

"He adores you, Ames. He always has."

"Yeah." I close my eyes and bask in the thought of him. "How are you doing?"

"I'm good," she responds, sighing. "I think it's these moments that I will miss the most. The time spent with family."

"Oh, Mom, please don't talk like that," I mutter, choking back tears. I've never been the best at dealing with death, especially with it being my mom.

"But it's true. I know it's not easy to talk about what's to come, but I think I'm coming to terms with it," she says. "Do you remember Silvia?"

"Yeah, of course. She was your good friend."

"When she was dying, she told me that the closer you come to death, the easier it is to accept. I never believed it, but the past week I've started to understand it."

"I'm not sure how I'm going to cope without you. I don't think I can get through life without you by my side."

"Sweetie, don't worry, you will. I'll be reunited with your dad. He was my rock for forty-six years, and it's been a long year without him."

"I love you," I say, trying to be strong for her.

"You are my world, Ames. I love you so much." She extends her hand. We lie in silence, holding hands.

After our massage is over, we spend the rest of the morning getting a facial and finish up before lunch with a manicure and pedicure. We decide to have lunch on the waterfront, enjoying the warmth of the sun.

"How's work?"

"It's not bad. Matthew and I have a trial that starts next week."

"Is that the one you mentioned?"

"It is. We have a strong case for self-defense. Matthew worked hard on this one."

"Is he lead council?"

"Yeah, I let him have this one. With everything that I've been dealing with lately, I haven't been able to give the trial prep the attention it needs. And to be honest, I'm happy he is. I haven't had the desire that I did before finding out about everything. A big part of me feels like I don't deserve the firm. I believe Marla and Drew always resented the fact that Dad left the firm to me, and, well, they might be right."

"Don't say that, Ames. You deserve it. You're such a great attorney. And the success that you've brought to the firm over the past year has been remarkable. Please don't ever doubt yourself."

"I don't feel that way."

"I'm incredibly proud of you. And the fact that your dad left the firm to you means nothing; you would still be this successful regardless. Don't ever think otherwise."

"No one can ever put things into perspective like you can. I'm going to miss these talks."

We finish lunch and she's reached her limit of fun for the day. We head back home so she can rest. I pull into the driveway and Drew and Travis' cars are both here.

"Did you know they were going to be here today?"

"No," she says, shaking her head.

After I help her out of the car and up the stairs, I open the door and we're immediately welcomed with the smell of something cooking in the kitchen. Drew saunters out of my dad's old office.

"Hi, Mom," he says, hugging her.

"What are you doing here? I thought you were working today?"

"Come with me. I have a surprise for you."

He takes my mom's hand and leads her through the entryway. Travis emerges from the kitchen with a bright smile.

"Hi there, pretty ladies," he says, kissing my mom on the cheek. He walks over to me, and after taking me in his arms, he kisses me.

"I didn't know you were going to be here," I say excitedly. Smiling, he takes my hand and we follow Drew into my dad's old office.

Stopping at the door, my mom puts her hand over her mouth. The office that was once filled with a huge mahogany desk, filing cabinets, and shelves has been transformed into a room of relaxation. The old furniture has been replaced with my mom's beautiful four poster bed, an overstuffed chair, a massage table, a dresser, television, and even a cot for someone to sleep on overnight. The sun shines through the windows and it looks inviting.

"You guys did this?" she asks, tears streaming down her face. I look at Travis in sheer wonderment, while I feel a lump form in my throat.

"Travis and I thought you'd be better down here, next to the kitchen. And the sun shines directly into the room with the window shades open."

My mom grabs hold of both Travis and Drew and hugs them. "You boys are incredible. Thank you."

DECEPTION

"We love you, Mom."

I watch them from the door. And while it's so beautiful what they've done for her, the thought of what's soon to come hits me hard. I need to walk away because I'm about to break down.

Rushing to the bathroom, I shut the door behind me and slide myself down the wall. I fall to the floor, and cry for all of the emotions that I'm experiencing. My mom doesn't realize how much she's going to be missed, and Drew and Travis don't realize how much they've made my mom happy.

Hearing a knock on the door, I take in a shaky breath and wipe the tears from my face. "One minute," I croak.

"Amy, are you okay?" Travis asks.

I open the door and he reaches for me as soon as he sees me crying. After pulling him in, he closes the door behind him.

"It's going to be all right."

"I'm going to miss her so much," I cry into his shoulder.

"I know," he says, hugging me and running his hand through my hair.

"I'm sorry. I don't want to take away from what you and Drew did. You guys made her so happy."

"We're glad to do this for her. Please don't cry, Sweets."

I finally catch my breath and hug him harder. He rubs my back, and his touch helps to calm me. After a few moments, I pull away.

"Thank you."

He gazes at me and smiles. "Do you realize that you're beautiful when you cry?"

I let out a small laugh. "I can imagine how I look right now, and beautiful isn't the word I'd use to describe it."

"I'm serious, you're so beautiful."

I kiss him, and he reciprocates.

We return to the home office, and I go over to my mom, who's now sitting in the chair, and hug her.

"Don't cry, honey," she says, squeezing me.

They are also cooking meals for her, for the next couple of days. Drew has to return to work, so he tells my mom that he'll be back around six o'clock to stay with her for the night. After he leaves, my mom asks me to get her book from the living room so she can read in the sun for a bit. After I retrieve it, I go to the kitchen to see if Travis needs my help.

"What can I do?"

"I think most of it is done. Anyway, I'm not sure I can focus much with you in the kitchen wearing that dress," he says, looking me up and down with a clever grin.

"I can go change into sweats, if you'd prefer."

"Not sure that would make much of a difference," he says, shuffling over to me. He wraps his arms around me and I snuggle in closer.

"Thank you for everything."

"I wouldn't have it any other way."

My mom coughs from the other room, and Travis tenses up in my arms.

"How about you go relax with my mom for a bit. I can finish up in here."

"Are you sure?"

"Yes, go. Plus, this kitchen is too hot with you in it," I say, winking.

He grins. "I think that's because you're in that dress," he says, leaning in for another kiss.

I coax him out of the kitchen. He heads in to visit with my mom, bringing her a glass of water. I absorb myself in cooking, and then wash the dishes once everything is done.

After making my way to the room to see what they would like to eat for dinner, I stand at the door and I'm stopped dead in my tracks. My mom is lying in her bed, and Travis is sitting in the chair, reading the book to her. My mom's hand is holding his arm and her eyes are closed. She looks content. I think I just fell in love with him all over again.

I don't think he can see me from where he's sitting so I remain there, looking in and listening to him as he reads. Resting my head against the door jamb, I wonder what I did to deserve him back in my life. He's so miraculous inside and out. I stare at him while he simply takes my breath away.

He glances up from the book and smirks but doesn't stop reading. He's caught me staring at him, but I don't care because I can't look away while my heart worships him. He reaches the end of a chapter and puts the book down, looking at my mom who has fallen asleep. He gazes at her with so much admiration, while he reaches over and squeezes her hand.

Looking up at me, he smiles. "How long were you going to stand there?"

"I could stand here looking at you all day." He extends his hand, and I walk over to him. "I'm convinced that you don't realize how wonderful you are."

Shaking his head, he sets the book on the bedside table. Standing up, he leans in. "You have to stop looking at me like that. You don't realize what that does to me," he whispers in my ear, and it sends a chill down my body.

DECEPTION

Taking my hand, he leads me out of the room and into the kitchen. Pressing me up against the wall, he kisses me with so much intensity. He runs his hand down my back, to my waist, and pulls me in closer. Slipping his hand down to my hip, he runs it along my thigh, pulling my dress up slightly. I can feel his desire build up. His touch captivates me. He pulls his mouth from mine, kissing my jaw and then my neck. While he kisses my collarbone and the part of my chest that's exposed from my dress, I run my fingers along the muscles of his back. I lose myself in the moment. Returning his mouth to mine, he explores my mouth with his tongue. We continue to lose ourselves in each other for a few more minutes.

"This is what you do to me," he whispers, trailing kisses from my mouth to my ear. He looks at me, smiling, and then inhales deeply. "I think you need to go put those sweats on. I'm not sure I can handle this dress on you much longer."

I laugh.

My mom coughs from the other room and we both tense, concern immediately rushing through me. This cough sounds different than the ones she's had the past couple days.

We hurry to the room while my mom continues to cough and gasp for breath. Travis rushes to her and rubs her back, while I reach for a towel on the bedside table. I hand it to her and she coughs into it. When I see that she's coughed up blood, I look at Travis, worried.

"It's okay, Mom. Let it out," Travis says calmly, while he rubs her back.

After her coughing subsides, I hand her a glass of water. She lies back on the bed in exhaustion. She reassures us that she's feeling better. But I don't want to leave her alone so I sit on the chair next to her and hold her hand, while she drifts back to sleep. I look at Travis, speechless. This is what the doctor was talking about when he said she may need assistance if she starts coughing. I feel like she's getting worse by the day. It's all happening too quickly.

Travis walks over to me and squats down next to the chair "Are you okay?" he asks, rubbing my arm.

"Yeah, I am now. That was so bad."

"Can I make you some dinner?"

"Sure," I say, nodding.

He kisses me on the cheek, and then heads into the kitchen. I look over at my mom, who's sleeping peacefully again. I'm not ready to let her go. And I don't know how I'm going to get through life without her.

Ten minutes later, Travis comes in holding two plates. After handing me one, he pulls a chair over next to me. He's made spaghetti and meatballs and it tastes divine.

"It's a good thing you didn't pursue engineering," I say, teasing. "You are quite the chef."

"I've learned a lot over the years," he says, raising an eyebrow.

Drew walks in. "How is she doing?"

"Well, she's been sleeping most of the time you were gone. But she had a coughing spell and it produced blood this time," I say, worried.

"Oh."

My mom wakes up from her nap, and Travis offers to get them both a plate of food. The rest seems to have helped her regain her energy from her busy morning, and the color in her face has returned—for the time being anyway.

When Travis returns from the kitchen, he glances at the time and announces that he has to leave to go pick up Amanda from her friend's house. I frown. Time with him never seems to be long enough. Going over to my mom's bedside, he hugs her.

"Thank you for everything you've done today. I love you so much, sweetie," she says, squeezing his hand.

"I love you, Mom. I plan to stop by tomorrow. Have a good night's rest."

He taps Drew on the shoulder. "Take it easy. I'll catch up with you later. Call me if you should need anything."

Drew stands and hugs him, and it makes me happy to see the two of them getting along so nicely. They got along really well when we were kids. They would always go fishing, and even to parties, while Travis and I were together. Drew never really created that bond with Rich—they never seemed to be on the same page. This is refreshing.

"I'll see you out," I say, taking Travis' hand and walking out of the room. I rest my head on his shoulder when we reach the front door, not wanting to let go of him. "I wish you didn't have to go," I say, pouting.

He sighs. "I know. I have to go into work tonight after I pick her up too. We're hosting a wedding tomorrow, and they want to decorate tonight. You could come with me."

"I really need to get a few things from my house. And I want to stay a bit with my mom after the afternoon she's had."

"It's okay, I understand."

"Thank you for everything today. You've made my mom so happy. I can't explain to you what that means to me," I say, stretching up on my toes and kissing him.

"You mean so much to me, Sweets. And your mom means a lot to me as well. I know that seeing her this way is difficult, but we'll get through it together." He shakes his head and looks me in the eyes with so much passion. "I adore you so much."

I tighten my arms around him. "I… I adore you too," I say, trying to choose my words wisely. I really want to tell him that I love him, but I'm scared that it may be too soon. It may even push him away, so I decide to keep that bit of information to myself for now. But boy do I love this guy.

He plants a soft kiss on my lips and then pulls away, scanning his eyes down my body. He shakes his head. "Hmm, that dress," he says, grinning. "I really have to go. That dress is dangerous," he adds, opening the front door.

I smile. "I'll make a note of that."

Once he leaves, I go in to see my mom.

"It's nice having him around again," Drew says.

"Yeah. I've been enjoying it a lot."

"He's such a sweet guy," my mom remarks endearingly.

"I'm happy for you, Amy," Drew adds.

"Thanks."

I tell them that I'm going to get some more things from my house, and that I'll be back shortly. The moment I get into my car, my phone dings. It's a text from Travis: *I've figured out that it's not so much the dress that's dangerous, but it's those incredible legs.*

I grin. I love that boy.

chapter twelve

Tuesday
April 30, 2013
1:42 p.m.

I tap Matthew on the shoulder. "You did great today. You nailed that opening statement. I couldn't have done a better job even if I tried. You've got this."

"Thanks, Amy. I hope you're right."

"You know my record of predictions. Trust me, you got this one. I'm proud of you," I say, hugging him.

For the past seven years I've predicted how the trial will go after the first day in court, and I've only been wrong twice. This case is Matthew's first big one as lead council. I've mentored him for the past three years.

He's even become like my little brother in some ways. I was hesitant to put him as lead council, but after what I witnessed I'm certain that I made the right choice.

"I learn from the best," he says, shooting me a grin.

We pack up and meander out of the courtroom.

"Attorney Silver," a woman calls out. I stop and scan the hallway to find a tall, blonde woman rushing in my direction. She looks like a reporter.

"Walk faster and don't look in her direction. Just walk toward the door," I advise Matthew.

"Attorney Silver," the woman calls again. "Excuse me, Amy, can I have a moment of your time?" I don't look in her direction, but her voice gets closer. Suddenly, I feel a hand on my arm.

"Sorry, we don't do interviews," I say, continuing to make my way to the doors, without looking at her.

"No, I'm not a reporter. I'm from the School of Law at the University of San Francisco, and I would like a moment of your time." USF? What would they want with me?

I stop and turn to her. Matthew waits for me. "What can I help you with?"

"Hi, I'm Lisa Brighton and I'm the head of the faculty in the School of Law at the University. I'd love to have a moment to talk to you about a potential teaching position."

"Sorry, I don't teach."

"I know you don't have experience teaching in the classroom. But we've been following your cases closely with our students, and the faculty and I all agree that you'd be a great addition to our team. We'd like the opportunity to sit down and speak with you about it."

"Well, I've never thought about teaching. If you want to leave me your card, I could call you at some point if it's something I think I'd be interested in."

"That would be wonderful," she says, reaching into her pocket and handing me her business card. "We have a professor that teaches criminal law who's retiring next month, so please do call. I think we could offer you something reasonable."

"Thank you," I say, shaking her hand before turning and walking out.

"Teaching, huh?" Matthew says, intrigued.

"Yeah. Not sure why they think I'd be good at teaching," I say, chuckling.

"It's evident you know what you're talking about. And they'd be lucky to have such a successful lawyer on their faculty. I don't blame them for wanting you."

"Or, maybe it's as the saying goes, 'Those who can, do. Those who can't, teach?'"

Matthew slaps me on the arm. "You know better than that."

"Ouch," I say, pushing him.

We arrive back at the firm, and Matthew gets the rock star treatment. The other attorneys already caught word about his great day in court.

Going over to Julie, I see a huge bouquet of pink roses sitting on her desk. "Is it your anniversary?"

"Hi, Amy. No, those aren't my flowers. Those were delivered for you. And they came with this." She hands me a large manila envelope. "We're dying to find out who they're from."

A card accompanies the flowers, so I open it to read: *Thank you*, and it's signed, *From Rich*

"You can keep them. They look great on your desk," I answer back, laying the card down and strolling to my office.

"What? Why? Who are they from?"

"Rich," I shoot over my shoulder.

"Oh no. I don't want them," she says, exasperated.

Sitting down, I'm curious as to what kind of surprise he's presented me with in the envelope—possibly another ridiculous contract? Or maybe it's an admittance of how big of a douche bag he is. I open it and take out a folded piece of paper that reads:

Amy,

I can't express to you how grateful I am that you allowed me to keep my firm. This is proof that I seriously don't deserve you.

Thank you,
Rich

I notice something else in the envelope. Reaching in, I take out a smaller envelope with *Ames* written on the top, and hearts drawn all over it. It's my mom's letter that she gave to me on my birthday. The envelope has been opened and resealed with tape. I shake my head.

Opening it up, I read the letter on the top:

My sweet Ames,

I recently came across some information that I think you should be made aware of. Before you read the attached, please know that

I love you so much and that's the reason that I've decided to tell you. After you read this, please call me so that we can talk. I have more details that I think will help to explain.

You will always be my sunshine,
Mom

I force a smile. I'm going to miss her. Flipping to the next page, I see it's a letter from my dad to Rich, on the law firm's letterhead. I scan through it and notice that it's the same letter that I've already read. But the second page is the official contract that Rich agreed to, something I haven't seen yet:

Official Contract

Mr. Richard Driscoll, known as "First Party," agrees to enter into this joint contract with Warren Silver Law Associates in San Francisco California and Reynard Enterprises in Cambridge, England, known as "Second Party" on June 10, 2011.

The invalidity or unenforceability of one or more provisions of this agreement shall not affect any other provision of this agreement. This agreement is subject to the laws and regulations of the state of California.

DECEPTION

This agreement is based on the following provisions:

Mr. Richard Driscoll agrees to spend the sum of $5 Million Dollars (to be wired) over the next five years in gifts and vacations to be presented to Amy Silver on her birthday and other occasions at his reasonable discretion, to include but not be limited to the following. In return Reynard Enterprises agrees to continue business connections with Mr. Richard Driscoll.

I glance down the page, starting to feel nauseated. There are well over thirty—or maybe even fifty—bullet points. I don't even want to put myself through the displeasure of reading it. Did my dad really do this? And Rich signed this? What the hell? This is sickening, and downright unheard of.

Grabbing the contract, I scurry over to the shredder. I watch it as it turns into tiny strands of paper, making this ridiculous agreement now a distant memory. It's evident that Rich is a jerk, but what man does this to his daughter? I will never be able to see it in a positive way like my mom has tried to convince me.

I saunter back to my desk and fish into my purse for my phone, wanting to text Travis to see how his day is going. Reaching into my bag, I accidentally grab the business card from Lisa Brighton, Esq.

Staring at it, I wonder what they have to offer and if I even want to teach. It's not something I've ever thought about. Flipping the card through my fingers, I lean back in the chair.

After a few minutes, I break myself from thought and decide to text my sister to see how my mom is doing instead.

Me: *How's Mom?*

Marla: *She's resting. She was able to eat some soup for lunch and has been able to hold it down so far.*

Me: *Good. I should be home in an hour or so. Do you need me to pick anything up on the way?*

Marla: *No. We're good. Maybe coffee would be nice though.*

Me: *Sure thing.*

I text my handsome boyfriend to see what he's doing.

Me: *Hey there, sexy!*

My handsome boyfriend: *Hey there, beautiful! I was just thinking about you. Of course, had you written me any other time, I would have been doing the very same thing. ☺ How was court?*

Me: *You know just what to say to a girl. ☺ Court was really good. Matthew hit it right out of the park.*

DECEPTION

My handsome boyfriend: *When are you coming home?*

Me: *Home? Do you mean my mom's house? I should be leaving work in an hour or so. Can you come by today?*

My handsome boyfriend: *I'm already here.*

Wait, he's at my mom's?

Me: *What are you doing there?*

My handsome boyfriend: *Just visiting, keeping her company.*

Me: *You're by far the sweetest man to ever walk this planet. What have I done to deserve you?*

My handsome—and incredibly sweet—boyfriend: *You're the one that told me this had nothing to do with luck, it is all fate. You and I were always meant to be, baby. Now get your incredibly sexy ass over here so I can smother you with kisses.*

Me (giddy): *Since you put it that way, I'm leaving right now!*

I turn off the computer, and while reaching for my bag, the business card sitting on my desk grabs my attention. A part of me is curious to see what they have to offer. I never thought about teaching, but who knows, it might be what I need to spike my motivation again. Taking hold of the phone, I dial the number.

chapter thirteen

*Friday
May 3, 2013
2:41 p.m.*

I've spent the last few days engrossed in the case. And today was especially difficult since our client took the stand. Listening to her speak about the night that changed her life forever—how the boy, who sat at the table beside us, had not only taken her virginity unwillingly, but had robbed her of being able to trust any other guy again—sent uncomfortable chills right down the center of my back. I rarely let cases get to me, but when we're representing a fifteen-year-old who has to recount details of being viciously raped, my body has a mind of its own. It's hard to separate yourself from it. And then I look over at the sixteen-year-old boy who did it to her—who has been left partially brain dead from her fight back with a tire iron—and it makes me want to cry for them all. I know I shouldn't want to cry for a boy who raped a girl—he got what he deserved—but it doesn't make me want to cry any less. Either practicing law is getting the best of me, or something inside of me is changing because I'm becoming more and more troubled by my clients' stories. I used to disconnect myself from them, especially in court. Maybe it's that I'm sitting second chair in this case and I'm able to listen more intently to the testimony. I don't know. But it feels different today. It feels sad.

"Good job," I say, patting Matthew on the shoulder. "You had a good week."

"Thanks. Let's hope we can wrap this up next week."

"Yeah."

We leave the courthouse and head back to the firm. I gather my messages from Julie, and slump down in my chair, spinning it around and around while staring into space. I have to snap out of this, it's so unlike me that I don't know how to respond to it. I need some cheering up and there is only one person that can do that for me right now, so I text Travis.

Me: *Hi*

Travis: *Hey there, beautiful girl. What are you up to?*

Me: *At work. Rough day in court. Needing some cheering up.*

Travis: *Everything okay? Want to call me?*

Me: *I'd rather see you. Seeing you would cheer me up. Where are you?*

Travis: *At work. Can you leave work and come?*

It is Friday, my day in court is over, the messages and emails can wait until Monday, and my aunt and sister are staying with my mom today. Nothing is standing in my way of going to see him. I could use a slice of the Love Shack right now.

Me: *Yes, and yes. I'm coming to you.*

I gather my things and tell Julie to head home. Laura walks out of her office as I'm leaving. "Hey, I haven't seen you all week. How are things going?"

"Good. It's been busy here this week. We took on two new cases, and they should be good ones."

"That's great. How's everything besides work?"

She shrugs. "Good, I suppose." It appears like she wants to say something more but decides not to. I'm sure her sister has made her life interesting in ways I have no desire to know.

"Good. Well, have a good weekend. Call me sometime so we can chat. I miss you," I say, hugging her. Since telling me about her sister and Rich, she's been distant. I imagine it must be difficult for her. I hope she knows that I still consider her a good friend, regardless of what happened.

Under an hour later, I walk into the Love Shack and a sense of relief washes over me. I never imagined a place—a bar none-the-less—could do this to me. Seeing my boyfriend talking with customers at the bar, I wander over. He's too busy talking to see me, so I sit a stool at the end of the bar, admiring the man before me. This is certainly what the doctor ordered to get me out of my slump. His laugh alone is the right medicine.

The bartender greets me, placing a napkin in front of me. "What can I get you, ma'am?"

"A red raspberry martini with Chambord, please." Travis instantly turns his head in my direction, his eyes meeting mine. A beautiful smile plasters his face, and it sends my heart racing around the track of the Daytona 500.

He quickly ends his conversation with the customers. "I got this," he tells the bartender.

He prepares my drink, while holding his gaze on mine the entire time, looking away long enough to pour the martini into the glass. He grabs a bottle of beer from the cooler and strolls over to me with our drinks in hand.

Making his way around the bar, he cocks an eyebrow and tilts his head, motioning for me to follow him. I oblige without hesitation. His gaze is mesmerizing. I'd follow him to the ends of the earth.

He leads us to my table on the patio. After setting our drinks down, he quickly turns to me, wrapping his arms around me.

"I missed you," he whispers, brushing his lips against mine. I breathe him in and kiss him passionately.

"Aren't I the lucky girl to be kissing the boss," I remark, slowly pulling away.

He smiles. "That's how we treat all of our VIP guests here at the Love Shack," he says, with a sly grin. I laugh.

"I don't even know the story behind why you called this place the Love Shack."

"Well, I'm hoping you don't want some grand love story because it's quite a boring reason. That was the name of the place before I bought it. I didn't change it because a lot of the residents in the area seemed to like

DECEPTION

it. I also wanted to continue hosting weddings out on the beach, like the previous owner did, so I thought it was appropriate. Sorry. Boring story, I know."

"It may be a boring reason but listening to you tell it is just as satisfying," I say, reaching up and kissing him again.

"Maybe I could change my story now though."

"What?" I ask, not following.

"I could say that the reason it's called the Love Shack is because this is the place I reunited with the love of my life," he responds, tilting an eye up and grinning. Wait a minute, did he just say he loved me without actually saying the three official words? I mean, is saying you're the love of my life the same as saying I love you? I don't know, but it sounds nice coming from him.

"I love that story much more."

Pressing his lips to mine, consuming my mouth, I melt in his arms.

He pulls my chair out. "Court wasn't good today?"

"The case is going good—really good. But I had a tough time listening to my client on the stand. This case is really affecting me personally, for some reason."

"Given the case, I can see why. You're only human for having an emotional response to it."

"I suppose you're right, but I've never reacted like this before," I say, dragging his chair close to mine and grabbing his hand. "I'm feeling better now, though."

"I'm really glad you're here. I actually have to be somewhere at four-thirty, and I would love for you to come with me."

I look at him, squinting. He winks in return.

"Where are we going?"

"I have to go see something in Half Moon." My heart sinks in response to his words. His parents lived in Half Moon, and I'm not sure what he would want to go there for after all that has happened.

"Oh—Kay," I say hesitantly.

"No worries, Sweets. I can sense what you're thinking. Where we're going is all good," he consoles, rubbing my arm.

"All right. I'll go wherever, as long as it's with you."

We finish our drinks, while enjoying the breeze of the ocean in each other's arms. Getting up from the table, Travis takes my hand in his and we walk over to the bar. He tells some guy that he's leaving for the day and asks him to call when he locks up tonight.

When we get outside, he holds the car door open for me and then climbs into the other side behind the wheel.

Twenty-five minutes later, we're in Half Moon. We pull up to a beautiful house that has a for sale sign in the large front yard. I look at him, narrowing my eyes. "You're buying a house?"

He grins. "Possibly."

"This looks like a really nice place," I say, peering out the window. It looks to be an old, restored home, with a lot of character on the outside. I'm taken aback because you don't find many of these types of homes in California. It's quite breathtaking.

"Yeah, wait until you see the inside."

When we exit the car, a woman approaches Travis. "Mr. Cashman, nice to see you again," she says, shaking his hand.

Travis introduces us, and then she leads us up the long stone walkway and up the stairs onto a wide, stone porch that wraps around two sides of the house. A green wooden swing hangs on one side and thoughts of spending time swinging with my grandmother on her porch as a kid flood my memory.

The woman unlocks the door and motions for us to go in. Standing in the entryway, I'm left speechless. The most gorgeous wood lines the floors and the walls are painted in a clay color, giving off a calming feel. The living room is lined with large windows, inviting the sun through them.

"This is really nice, Travis," I say, awe-struck.

"I can't wait for you to see this kitchen," he says, tugging on my arm. We walk in and my jaw drops. The kitchen in my house pales drastically in comparison. Stone covers the wall around the large stove, and the rest of the walls are lined with beautiful cream cabinetry. Even the floor is stone.

"Wow," I say, excitedly.

"I'll leave you two to wander around. I'll be outside if you should need me," the woman says.

"Thanks," Travis responds, nodding.

I walk around the kitchen, running my fingers across the marble countertops in complete amazement. I never imagined I'd be drawn to a house like this before.

"Come check out the upstairs," he says, reaching out for me to take his hand.

Standing at the top of the stairs, I look into the bedroom. Large windows line the back wall that overlooks a large backyard, with nothing but the woods beyond it. On the wall to the right is a beautiful stone fireplace. And the floors are lined in hand scraped hardwood. It's stunning.

He takes my hand and leads me to the master bath. The entire room is in white, with a stone lined shower and matching floors. And in the corner sits a beautiful claw footed tub.

"This is incredible."

"I'm glad you like it because I bought it," he says, wrapping his arm around my shoulders.

"You did?" I say, shocked and impressed.

"I'm signing the papers on Monday."

"What made you decide to buy a house in Half Moon? I mean, your bar is in Pescadero and I thought Amanda liked it there?"

"Yeah, but she's been missing her friends in Half Moon. She's been spending a lot of time here lately, and she's expressed that she'd like to come to high school here next year so—"

"Well, that makes sense."

"And it's closer to San Francisco," he says, grinning.

"You'll be closer to me. That's always a plus."

"And, well, maybe someday, you would want to move in," he says, shrugging and attempting to gauge my reaction. His words both scare and comfort me—at least that's what I think these emotions are that I'm feeling. "Does that scare you?" he inquires hesitantly. I contemplate his question, and realize that it's not fear I feel, it's more uncertainty.

"No, not scared. But I can't help but think what moving in with someone resulted in for me. I can't say that I've had a good experience with moving in with a guy," I respond, looking down reflectively.

He places a hand on both sides of my head, tilting my eyes up to his. "Don't ever think that you and I will turn out like you and him. I know that you may be scared of what may come of us, but we share something that people rarely get the chance to experience in their entire lives. If life has reunited us after all of these years, you have to know that we're meant to be." His words reach into my chest and speak directly to my slow beating heart. He whispers into my ear, "I love you, Sweets." My heart jumps out of my chest and starts doing the cha-cha right there on the beautiful stone floor.

I swallow hard. "I'm sorry, I didn't hear what you said. What was that?"

"I love you so much, Sweets. I've loved you since I can remember, and I will love you for eternity," he whispers, not moving his head from my ear.

Chills run up and down my body, causing goose bumps from both his words and the feel of his breath on my ear. I'm filled with so much desire and love for this man holding me. I turn my head to his and can see the passion flood his eyes.

"I'm glad you said that because I was afraid I was the only one feeling that way. I've wanted to tell you that I love you for a while, but I was scared I'd push you away. But hearing those words spoken from you makes me want to yell it on the roof tops. I love you, Trav. I love you so much."

He puts his lips to mine and kisses me with so much hunger. This kiss feels different than all the others before them. I push up against him harder, feeling like he's not close enough—like I need to jump inside his body or it won't feel close enough. Our hands explore each other, our mouths consume each other, and our breathing is in sync with each other's. I've missed this man so much that I don't want to live another day without him.

"I love you, Travis Cashman. I love you," I say in panted breaths.

Those words seem to spark his desire for me even more. He pushes me up against the wall, while running his hands through my hair, down my back, and down the back of my thighs pulling my legs up around his waist. We get lost in each other.

Quite a while later, he slowly pulls his mouth away, taking in deep breaths and releasing them. He looks at me for a moment, and then he closes his eyes, appearing to attempt to find his composure. We stand in silence as we both try to come back down from our complete rapture.

"Damn, Sweets, I've missed you. I've waited so many years to hear those words from you. You are incredible," he says, through exhaled breaths.

"You and I were always meant to be, baby," I say, quoting him from the other day.

He nods slowly. "Forever."

He kisses me on the corner of my mouth, and then leisurely lowers me back down to the floor. "I guess we like this bathroom," I say, grinning.

"I can imagine how we end up liking this bedroom once I'm moved in," he says, wide-eyed.

"And... when I move in," I add confidently, without a second thought.

chapter fourteen

Sunday
May 5, 2013
7:32 a.m.

I wake to the sound of my mom moving around. Sitting up on the cot, I see her struggling to get up from the bed so I rush to her side.

"Do you need to go to the bathroom?" I ask, panicked. She nods.

Her ability to speak has diminished the past few days. She tries to speak but ends up in tears instead. She's also pale and weak, barely able to sit up on her own, let alone stand and walk. It's becoming more difficult for us to care for her. Drew arranged for a visiting nurse to come to the house, but she won't be starting until tomorrow.

I stand by her side, put one arm around her waist, and she grabs my hand as I pull her up off of the bed. Taking slow, cautious steps, we make our way to the bathroom.

I return her to the bed after she's finished. She lies down and exhaustion sets in. After closing her eyes, she drifts back to sleep as soon as I hear the front door close. What time is it? Drew is early. He's not supposed to be here until eight o'clock to stay with her while I go to church. I haven't been to church for a few weeks, and this will be the first time going without my mom. You'd think it wouldn't bother me as much as it is—it's only church after all. But this was our Sunday tradition—me and my mom—and going without her doesn't feel right. I know that she'd be happy if I did, so I will.

Travis appears in the doorway. He's wearing a black suit, a white button-down dress shirt, and a beautiful burgundy tie. He looks delicious.

I narrow my eyes. "What are you doing here?"

He shrugs and winks. "Going to church," he says, walking over to me. A huge sense of relief rushes over me.

I wrap my arms around his neck and hug him. "Thank you."

"I could sense you were struggling with the thought of going without Mom when you told me about it yesterday. I couldn't let my girl go it alone," he says, planting a kiss in my hair.

"You have no idea what that means to me," I say, cradling his face in my hands and kissing him.

"How's Mom?" he whispers.

I shrug with a saddened expression. "Weak. I had to take her to the bathroom, and she could barely walk."

He looks over at her with concern. "I'll sit here with her while you get ready."

"Thank you. Drew should be here soon."

⊗ ✺ ⊘

We sit in church, listening to the sermon. Travis holds my hand the entire time and rubs my arm. This wasn't as bad as I envisioned. I'm sure having him here with me has helped.

The service ends, and we get back in the car just as Travis' phone rings.

"It's Amanda," he says, answering it. He talks for a bit and then hangs up.

"Is everything all right?"

"She's fine. She and a couple of friends want to go hiking today. They have to do a nature walk for school.

She was asking if I could bring her. Are you up for a hike today?"

"Yeah, sure," I respond, excited. I haven't been hiking in a long time. I once really enjoyed it. Rich wasn't into nature—actually he wasn't into the outdoors, at all—and my friends are more of the beach babes. "I need to change my clothes first, though."

"I agree. I don't think I'd be able to hike much with you in that dress. That would be a recipe for trouble, considering Amanda will be with us." Shit, that's right, Amanda's going to be there. This is the first time I'll meet her. Not that I don't want to meet her, I really do. But now that the time has come, I'm a bit nervous about it. I hope she likes me. I know that would mean the world to Travis.

He puts his finger under my chin, tilting my head in his direction. "I know what you're thinking, and I can see the worry on your face. You girls will hit it off."

"I know," I say, but not sure I'm even convincing myself of it.

"I promise," he says, taking my hand in his and kissing it.

We drive back to my mom's house. While he visits with my mom and Drew, I get changed into shorts and a tank top and put my hair up into a bun.

DECEPTION

I go back downstairs to tell him I'm ready. I see Drew in the kitchen, so I go to my mom's room and I'm frozen in place. Travis is sitting on the edge of the bed and my mom is leaning into him, while resting her head on his shoulder. Travis has both arms around her and he's swaying her to the music, both of them with their eyes closed. The love that this man has to give is simply breathtaking to witness. I can't help but watch from the doorway. The song ends and my mom raises her head, kissing him lightly on the cheek. Travis hugs her. He peeps in my direction, and I put one hand over my heart and blow a kiss to him with the other. He smiles.

Propping pillows behind her, he tells her that Drew will be in shortly with some lunch. She grabs his hand and kisses it. "Thank you," she mouths.

I go over and hug her, reassuring her that we'll be back later. Before heading out, I tell Drew to call us if he should need anything.

Travis pulls me to him and whispers, "I'm not sure those shorts are much better than the dress." I smile. He looks at me with raised eyes. "Maybe this hiking thing isn't a good idea after all."

I tug his arm and pull him into me, kissing him. "We could always explore other things if you'd prefer," I murmur.

He shakes his head and closes his eyes for a brief moment. "It's a good thing that Amanda needs to do this for school because that sounds so appealing. Can I take a rain check?" he whispers in my ear. The feel of his breath makes me shudder. I nod and lean in to kiss his neck.

An hour later, we're in Pescadero picking up Amanda and her two friends. Travis introduces me to them as they pile into the car. I'm struck with how beautiful Amanda is. I recognize so many features of her mom. I notice that her face, arms, and hands have scarring, but, regardless, she's really quite stunning.

"Hi, Amy," she says, reaching her hand out. Wow, and so polite too.

"It is so nice to meet you, Amanda," I say, taking her hand.

Travis tells her and her friends that we need to make a stop at his house so he can change. He grabs my hand in his, resting it on his leg as he drives off. The girls giggle in the backseat. Travis glances in the rearview mirror and winks at Amanda. It's like they have their own secret language that doesn't need to be spoken. I squeeze his hand, sending my heart aflutter.

He looks at me and smiles. The girls giggle even louder, and he grins.

When we pause at a red light, they're easily distracted by a boy in the car next to us, quickly bringing them back to their teenage girl ways. "Are they always like this?" I whisper.

He chuckles. "No. But they've also never seen me with a girl, so I really wouldn't know."

"Amanda has never seen you with anyone? Like, no one from your past relationships?" I ask, shocked.

He shakes his head. "Nope. No one's been worthy of bringing around." Amazed by his words, I sit in silence. All these years and he's never brought any woman to his house or around Amanda, but he's been so anxious for us to meet.

We arrive at his house and the girls run in, announcing they need to use the restroom and want something to drink. "I'll only be a minute," he says, kissing my cheek.

Moments later, he emerges from the bedroom in a fitted t-shirt and cargo shorts, and he looks damn hot. I cock an eyebrow and grin. He bites down on his lower lip, knowing what I'm thinking. The girls come out of the kitchen with bottles of water and snacks.

"Would you like a bottle of water?" Amanda asks.

"That would be great. Thanks," Travis replies.

She returns to the kitchen and brings back two bottles, handing one to each of us.

"Thank you," I say, taking it. She smiles in return.

After piling back into the car, we drive for a bit. "Remember this place?" he asks, pulling up to a hiking trail in San Mateo.

"Yes, of course," I say, enthusiastic. This was one of our favorite hiking spots, and the one where Travis gave me my promise ring. Taking my hand in his, he pulls it up to his mouth, kissing my ring. The girls snicker in the back seat.

When we get out of the car, Amanda laces her arm in mine. "Come with us," she says to me. My mouth forms a smile, but my heart smiles bigger. I glance over at Travis who is, by far, smiling the widest.

We start climbing the trail while the girls pause to pick up leaves and rocks. Giggling and talking, they walk a bit in front of us, leaving Travis and I to ourselves. Travis slows down and tells the girls not to go too far ahead without us. Finding a large rock, he directs me to sit. Sitting by my side, he puts his feet up on the rock. The view from here is perfect. We can see into the city above all the trees.

I rest my head on his shoulder and he puts his arm around me. "She's beautiful," I remark, looking at Amanda with her friends.

"Yeah, she is. But she's even more beautiful on the inside. Her kindness amazes me sometimes."

"That's proof that she's been raised well. You should be proud of yourself for that. Her kindness is much like your own." He squeezes me.

"She may have taught me, instead of me teaching her."

"Not possible, you've always been this way."

Reaching into his pocket, he pulls out his phone. "We need a new picture for the wall at the bar," he says, smiling.

He calls for Amanda to take a picture of us. She runs to us, smiling, and grabs his phone. He wraps both arms around me and kisses me while she takes the picture.

"Can you take a picture with my phone, too?" I ask her. She nods excitedly. I hand it to her and we reenact the first picture.

"Thanks," I say when she hands me back the phone.

"You're welcome," she responds, endearingly. "Can we go up to the top of the trail?" she asks Travis.

"Do you have your phone on you?" he asks. She nods. "All right but be careful."

Deciding that I want our new picture to be my wallpaper on my phone, I attempt to figure out how to save it. In doing so, my finger slides over the screen accidentally and I immediately feel nauseated. "Oh no!" I exclaim.

"What's the matter?" Travis asks with concern.

"Can you delete a picture from my phone for me? I can't look at it enough to remove it."

Narrowing his eyes, he takes my phone. "Okay."

"You'll know which one it is when you see it."

He slides his finger on the screen, and the look of shock floods his face. He stares down at it and then over to me. "This is the picture you took when you caught them together?" I nod in disgust. "Um, is this the kind of stuff you're into as well?"

I gasp. "Hell no. Oh goodness, no." I let out a snort.

"Good. I don't think I have it in me to do that."

"Please delete it. I don't want that on my phone. I don't even know why I took it in the first place."

He presses a few things and tells me that it's gone, passing the phone back to me. "Are you sure that's not what you like?" he asks hesitantly.

I slap his arm. "Trav, please. No. No way. I had no idea that he was even into that."

"All right. Good," he says, trying to sound convinced. "So why didn't you guys ever get married?"

DECEPTION

"Hmm... well, neither one of us ever wanted to do the whole marriage and kid thing."

He shakes his head. "That's not really true. You can't say you never did. I remember you and I talking about getting married and having three kids someday. You know, the whole house and white picket fence thing."

I think. Yeah, I guess I did want that at one point in my life, with Travis. I had forgotten about that until this moment.

"Yeah, I guess you're right. But after going through what we did all those years ago, I had sworn off all guys. I wanted nothing to do with them because I convinced myself that they were all lying, cheating bastards. I never even dated for so many years. I had no interest. Then I met Rich at one of my dad's functions and I wasn't into him at first, I actually thought he was arrogant and annoying. He kept coming around, and he grew on me. We started spending more time together. I'm not sure how or when it came up, but he stressed that he wasn't the marrying type. I don't know if that's what made me feel the same way, or maybe I felt he wasn't the right one, but either way I never wanted marriage and kids with him," I say, shrugging. "How about you? Did you ever find someone you wanted to marry?"

He presses his lips in a tight line and shakes his head. "No. I had a few relationships, but they never lasted long. I always held out hope that I'd find someone who I felt was the one for me—someone I didn't get tired of or find flaws in after three or so months—but I never did. I've had six short relationships—if you even want to call it that—over the years. None came close to making me feel fulfilled and satisfied. Not even close. I'm convinced that everyone has one true love—one soul mate—in life, and I met mine at the age of fifteen."

"I love you," I say, kissing him.

The girls return from their hike, announcing that they're done gathering what they need. We walk back down to the car. I hold Travis' hand and Amanda hangs onto his other arm. The smile on his face couldn't be brighter.

We drive back to Pescadero and drop them off at Amanda's friend's house. "It was nice to finally meet you," Amanda says, getting out of the car.

"It was so nice to meet you too," I reply, fixating on one word that she spoke—finally.

She leans in and kisses Travis' cheek, and then tells him that she'll see him after school tomorrow.

DECEPTION

After she walks into the house I turn to Travis. "When did you tell her about me?" He looks at me with knowing eyes.

"She's known about you for some time, at least a year, since your mom contacted me. She saw your picture at the bar years ago, though. I had to tell her about us, it's my favorite thing to talk about," he says, squeezing my hand and then backing out of the driveway.

We get to San Francisco and pull into my mom's driveway. "Do you want to come in and we can make some dinner?" I ask, not wanting him to go.

"Sure," he says quickly.

We head inside and check in on my mom. Drew made her dinner and she's eating. My sister is in the kitchen throwing together some pizzas, so I help her out. Drew offers Travis a beer, and they return to my mom's room.

"I know I haven't told you yet, but I love that you guys are back together," Marla says.

"Thanks. I do too."

"You guys are just right for each other. I've always thought that."

We eat and watch a movie with my mom. Drew leaves and my mom settles in for the night. I tell Marla to stay and relax with her, and I'll get the dishes and kitchen cleaned up. Travis helps.

Afterward, he hesitantly announces that he should leave since both of us need to be up early in the morning. I sulk and hang onto him, not wanting him to go, but knowing that he has to. We walk to the front door, passing by my mom's room. The television is turned off and Marla is reading by the bedside light. She waves good-bye to Travis.

Strolling to the front door, I'm still pouting. He pulls me in for a kiss and I don't want to let go, I don't want to stop. I wrap myself around him and enjoy the feel of him up against me.

"Call me when you get out of court tomorrow?" he asks. I nod, still sad that I have to let him go.

"I love you so much, baby," I say pulling him in for another kiss. "Thank you for a wonderful day."

"This was such a great day. I'm so glad that Amanda got to meet the love of my life," he responds. "I love you, Sweets."

Opening the front door, we notice that it's raining—quite hard. He looks at me with a playful, terrified look on his face. I laugh.

"Good luck," I joke. He smiles.

DECEPTION

"Good night, Sweets," he says, pulling his hand from mine while stepping onto the porch.

I watch him as he slowly walks backwards down the stairs, keeping his gaze on mine. The rain starts to slather him, but he doesn't react, he keeps walking while looking at me. He extends both arms straight out to his sides with his hands up, and he spins around in the rain. He looks like he's enjoying it. Seeing him soaked from the rain makes him look so irresistible.

Unable to contain myself, I run onto the porch and down the stairs, right into his arms. I jump up and wrap my legs around his waist, and he holds me up as I put my mouth on his. The feel of the rain and his mouth consume me. I'm convinced that I don't want him to go.

I lean in. "Stay with me tonight?"

"I'd like that," he says, pulling me in for another kiss. I attempt to wiggle down out of his hold, but he tightens his grip on me and walks back in the direction of the house. He carries me through the front door and closes it behind us.

He carries me upstairs to my room, with our mouths still locked on each other's. He lowers me down onto the bed, and then returns to the door to close and lock it. Returning to me, I pull on his shirt to get him to lower down on top of me, drawing his lips to mine again.

He pulls away slightly. "Are you sure you want to do this?" he asks, through panted breaths.

"I've never been so sure of anything," I say, drawing him back in. "Are you okay?"

"I'm so much more than okay," he says with so much desire in every word.

His tongue searches for mine while clasping his hands with mine on either side of my head. He trails kisses along my jaw line, to my ear, and down my neck, setting off the fireworks inside my body once again. He continues kissing my neck and down lower on my chest.

Wanting him to remove his clothing, I free my hands from his and tug on the bottom of his shirt. He leans back on his legs and allows me to pull it off. He grabs my shirt and I raise myself off of the bed enough for him to remove it. I lower myself back down, bringing him with me. He hovers his body over mine, pressing just enough into me. He kisses my chest and the center between my breasts, then down to my stomach, and a spark fires within me.

I reach down, wanting to remove all the layers of clothing that remain between us. I need to feel the warmth of his skin to mine, all of it. He pulls away enough to remove his shorts and underwear. He then unfastens the button on my shorts and slides them down my legs while he kisses my stomach and down to my thighs. He throws my shorts onto the floor and then places his fingers under the elastic of my underwear, pausing slightly before pulling them down and off me. He trails kisses back up my body and reaches behind me, unclasping my bra. He removes it, flinging it to the floor.

When he leans off the bed, stretching down to the floor, I instantly realize what he's searching for. "You don't need that. I'm—I'm on the—" but before I can finish, he's back on top of me, filling my mouth with his. I'm completely intoxicated by him. I've lost all ability to move or think.

When I feel like I'm going to completely lose it, he raises himself back on top of me and finds my mouth again. "I love you," he whispers.

After we spend a while longer losing ourselves in each other, he lowers himself down next to me, and I feel the rapid beat of his heart and it's in sync with mine. "You're incredible, Sweets. You are perfect—absolutely perfect for me," he says, breathing heavily.

"And so are you, Mr. Cashman. I love you," I say, wrapping my hands behind his neck. He props himself up on an elbow next to me and trails his fingers on my stomach. I can see his face in the moonlight that shines through the window and he looks amazing.

"Thank you, God, for leading my man back to me," I say, looking up at the ceiling. He chuckles. I'm reminded that no other guy has ever been in this bed.

"You've been the only one," I confess. He looks down at me puzzled. "The last time a guy's been in this bed, it was you."

He raises an eyebrow. "I like that," he says, amused. He shakes his head. "Wow, do I ever love you. Wow."

I snuggle up against him while thanking God—and my mom too—for bringing him back to me. Lowering himself down next to me, he stretches his arm behind my head. I lay my head down on his chest and he wraps his arms around me, holding me close, while we drift off to blissful sleep.

chapter fifteen

Wednesday
May 8, 2013
1:08pm

"Congratulations," I say to Matthew, hugging him.
"Thanks, Amy."
Matthew just won his first case as lead council. He presented his closing arguments this morning. The jury took less than thirty minutes to deliberate, before coming back with a not guilty verdict. There was no question in anyone's mind—including the jury's—that this was a self-defense case. I'm glad that it's over. Not only has this case affected me unexpectedly, but my mom has gotten so much worse the past couple of days.

She's no longer able to walk and she's been coughing up a lot of blood. I simply want to spend more time with her. I've decided not to take on any new cases so that I can devote my days to be with her since there are few left. Both Drew and Marla have been spending a lot of time with her as well, and so has Travis. He's been over every day for the past week or so now. He's even been there while I'm in court, to be by her side and help out any way that he can. It's been so endearing, and it makes me fall in love with him more and more with each passing day—if that's even possible.

Today marks the one-year anniversary of my dad's passing, and I've been struggling with the thought of paying him a visit. A part of me still feels like his baby girl, but another big part of me is angry with him. What could visiting his grave positively do for my emotions at this point? I don't see getting any closure from it.

I drive to my house to gather more clothes, and to check on things since I haven't been there in a week. I pull into the driveway and my new Lamborghini stares me in the face. It's been sitting here for many weeks now, unused. I don't see it the same way I did when I first got it. I feel disgusted simply looking at it.

I get out of the car and go inside the house. It feels empty and cold, despite every room being filled with furniture. It doesn't even feel like home. I don't think it ever really did. While it's a beautiful house—an excessively large house that is furnished with over-priced furniture—it doesn't feel right. I once thought that all of the grand and pricey materialistic things were what made me happy. I sure got slapped back into reality. I lived in this lavish home with a man who had no love for me, and I'd happily live in a straw hut with Travis for the rest of my life instead.

While gathering clothes from the bedroom, I decide to take my box of memories with me as well. This house isn't worthy of it. Not wanting to be there a moment longer, I walk out and close the front door behind me. Standing on the porch, looking at my new car, I know exactly what I want to do with it. After loading the clothes and the memory box into my Cadillac, I grab my cell phone and dial the Lamborghini dealership. I make arrangements to have it resold. They agree to come by to get it tomorrow. Relief and contentment set in at once.

After pulling out of the driveway, I decide to stop by the cemetery on my way to my mom's house. I have some things I need to get off my chest.

While I sit in front of my dad's grave in silence, I pick the weeds from the ground, contemplating what I want to say. "You know, I considered not even coming today. I've been so angry with you. I have so much I want to say—so much I'd want to ask if you were still here on earth with us, but I learned over the past month that none of the answers would matter. It's ironic that the one guy you pushed out of my life, is the same one who's been by Mom's side not only through her illness, but over the past year while she's been mourning and missing you. And the guy you practically forced to stay with me is the one who hasn't cared to be part of the family since you left. He hasn't even wanted anything to do with Mom at all. It makes me think that you'd rethink your plan had you known. I'd like to think so anyway."

I grow quiet for a while longer, trying to figure out if coming here was a good idea because I'm not feeling a sense of closure. I look at his headstone and see my mom's name engraved next to his, and my heart hurts knowing I'll soon be coming here to visit my mom as well. My name could even be there too.

"If Mom hadn't come home when she did that day thirteen years ago, finding me unconscious, I would have been the one waiting for you at heaven's gates. I'd be lying right here in the ground next to you. That was all because of you and your selfish agenda. Of all the people in the world I'd think that you would be the one to recognize true love. You and Mom were happily married since the age of twenty. Why you never wanted

DECEPTION

the same for your own daughter, I'll never know. If it's because of prestige and money, well Mom certainly doesn't come from a wealthy family and it was apparent that she had more love for you than anyone with wealth could ever have. And, well, if it's because your baby girl followed in your footsteps and wanted to study law as well, you may have pushed her away from that too. I met with the school of law yesterday and they offered me a teaching position that sounds appealing. Since learning about your master plan, I haven't felt the same about my career. I'm doing a lot of soul searching and, as a result, a piece of me feels like you may have willed me into this career path. I never wanted to disappoint my daddy, so I did it. I think you wanted this more for me than I did for myself. I just know that being at the firm and working cases doesn't have the same feel as it once did. Without Rich who was so career-driven and money hungry, and with Travis who has nothing but love to give me and a sense of security, it's allowed me to think about what I truly want in life. The big house, expensive cars, lavish vacations, and all the materialistic things that money can buy are not what matter to me. The way that Travis makes me feel, watching him with Mom and our family, and the sincere kindness that he possesses confirms to me that he's my true love. And that is what I want. So, no matter how hard you tried to keep us apart, you can't come between love, it'll always find a way back in. And, ultimately, your wife is the one to thank for it."

I plant a kiss on the headstone. "I will always love you and hope someday I can forgive you. Until then, rest assured that I'm happy, well taken care of, and loved."

I get up, brush myself off, and stroll to the car with a sense of new-found relief.

chapter sixteen

Saturday
May 11, 2013
8:51 a.m.

I get out of bed and follow the smell of coffee brewing, which leads me straight to the kitchen.

"Good morning, Marla," I say, walking over and pouring a cup.

"Hey there, Sis. How did you sleep?"

"Good. How about you? How was Mom last night?"

"She had a restful night. She woke up coughing once, but overall, she was good."

ISABELLE VAN BUREN

I've spent a good part of the last three days with my mom, who had a roller coaster of days. Even with the visiting nurse here, we still want to split up shifts for one of us to be with her at all times. As much as a nurse can do, there's nothing like the comfort of having your family by your side. And Mom certainly deserves it. Yesterday seemed to be her best day recently, so Drew and Marla convinced me to get some fresh air. Travis was busy at work doing inventory, so Laura and I did a bit of shopping and had lunch. And then we stopped by Tracy's salon to chat for a bit. It felt good to get out and unwind.

Today's a big day. It's my mom's sixty-eighth birthday tomorrow and we planned a surprise birthday party for her. Family and friends will be coming by for a BBQ this afternoon. I'm in charge of getting the cake and desserts from her favorite local bakery, Travis offered to bring food from his restaurant, Drew's going to cook, and Marla's going to decorate. My mom will be surprised to see everyone. We even have family coming in from out of town. I hope she has enough energy to get through the day.

"What time are you leaving to get to the bakery?" Marla asks, taking a bite of toast.

"I think I'll leave around nine-thirty. That should be plenty of time to get back and help decorate."

DECEPTION

I hear the front door open and close. Who could that be? I look at Marla questioningly. She shrugs.

After a few moments, no one makes an appearance so I wander down the hallway to see who it is.

I look into my mom's room and find Travis sitting on her bed, talking with her. What is he doing here so early? He's not supposed to be here for another couple of hours at least. He sees me looking in.

"Good morning, beautiful," he acknowledges.

"Hey there," I respond, not saying anything more, in an attempt not to give anything away to my mom.

He tells her that he'll see her later, and then he saunters over to me. He wraps his arms around me and kisses me.

"What are you doing here so early?" I whisper.

He smiles, and then takes my hand leading me into the kitchen.

"Good morning, Marla," he says when we enter.

"Hey, Travis."

"So, I figured you guys could use some extra help today."

"Sure," Marla quickly responds.

"Always willing to help. You are so sweet." His spontaneity is so refreshing.

He smiles in return. "So do you want me to take you to get the cake?" he asks.

"Sure."

"Are you ready now?"

"I suppose. I was trying to get my caffeine drip in," I joke.

"Come, we'll grab some coffee on the way. I actually forgot to stop at the Shack on my way here to get the food, so we'll need to take a drive there to get it. Is that okay?"

"Of course." Extra time with my man is always welcomed.

"See you guys in a bit," Marla says.

We walk out to the porch. "You took your Cadillac?" I say eagerly, the moment I see his 1972 Cadillac sitting in the driveway.

"I thought we could run errands in style today."

When we get in and start driving, Travis doesn't head in the direction of the bakery or the coffee shop. "We're getting the cake from the bakery on Morris," I say when I notice.

"I figure we can grab the food first and then get the cake. We can stop for coffee on the way."

"Sounds good to me," I say, grabbing his hand and snuggling in close to him. I love this car. It reminds me of when we were teenagers, making me a bit sentimental every time I'm in it.

DECEPTION

After stopping for coffee, we get onto the highway in the direction of the Love Shack. Fifty or so minutes later we pull up and Travis comes to my side of the car, opening the door. He takes my hand, meandering up to the front door, he pushes it open.

"It's unlocked?" I ask, surprised that it's open this early. We step foot inside the door and I'm struck with the view of what looks to be a field of sunflowers. I look up at Travis dumbfounded. He leans down and kisses me, and then squeezes my hand.

"What is this?" I manage.

He doesn't respond, instead he takes my hand and leads me to the center of the room. I take in the beauty around us. Every table is blanketed with sunflowers, and the bar is lined with bouquets of sunflowers as well. It's really magnificent.

Taking a chair, he places it in the center of the room. "Here, have a seat."

He then grabs another chair, and places it directly in front of me, sitting. Reaching over to the table next to us, he pulls a sunflower out of a vase and breaks off a piece of the stem. He places the sunflower in my hair. I'm speechless. Grabbing my hands in his, he leans in, resting his elbows on his knees.

"Do you know what today is?" he asks, peering into my soul.

I look at him, confused. "It's the day before my mom's birthday?"

"Today is our seventeenth anniversary," he says, grinning. "Six thousand, two hundred, and five days ago, we went on our first date. At the end of the date, I asked you to be my girlfriend. You've been in my heart ever since."

Tears well in my eyes. He grabs a tissue from what appears to be a strategically placed tissue box, and hands it to me.

"The moment I laid eyes on you, at the age of fifteen, I knew I had to have you as my girlfriend. The moment I placed that promise ring on your finger, I meant it to be forever. Every single moment that we've spent together, then and now, has been nothing but perfect. I was lost without you for thirteen years. You are the joy of my life. You are the air that I breathe. You are my one true love. You complete me." He pauses, taking in a breath. "At last, my soul mate has returned to me, so I'm wondering if you're willing to allow me to be your knight and light for life."

He reaches over to the table beside him and takes a sunflower in his hand. He gets down on one knee and holds it out to me. My body shakes as tears stream down my face. I can barely reach out to grab the flower with my trembling hand, but I manage. I look at it and see a tag hanging from it.

I read, through tear-stained eyes: *Will you marry me today?*

I pause, letting the words sink in. And then I read it again, making sure that I've read it correctly.

"Today?" I ask, barely forming the words. He nods.

"Yes. Sweets, will you give me the honor of becoming my wife today?"

I don't give it a moment's thought longer. "Yes," I say, leaping into his arms. He holds me tight and kisses me deeply.

"Let me explain why I've chosen today," he says once we pull away. "I've had a long time to dream about this day, but your mom has as well. Unfortunately, her days are limited. And the greatest gift I could give to you, and her, would be what we have planned for today."

I cradle my face in my hands. Travis leans over and brings me to him. He hugs me while I sit in his lap, crying.

"No matter how much longer we wait, it won't change my feelings for you. It won't diminish my need to spend eternity with you. You are my forever."

"I love you so much," I say in shaky breath. "So, we're getting married at my mom's today?"

"We're getting married here on the beach today," he says, swiping a tear from my eye.

"Here?" I question, both excited and surprised. "My mom is coming here too?"

"Your mom, our family, and our friends are all going to be here," he explains.

"Oh wait," he says, standing us up and reaching into his pocket. He pulls out a box and opens it to a stunning square cut diamond in a vintage setting. "You need this," he says, grabbing my left hand.

He pauses when he sees my promise ring on my ring finger, right where he placed it. He smiles, knowing that I never took it off, as I promised. He removes the promise ring and places it on the ring finger of my right hand, and then he slides the diamond ring onto the ring finger of my left hand. The diamond sparkles for all to see. It's simple, but so elegantly stunning.

"It's perfect."

"So, are you ready?"

"Ready? For what?"

"You have a big day planned," he says, grabbing my hand and walking me to the front door. When he opens the door, I'm met with Laura, Julie, Tracy, and Marla standing outside.

"She's all yours for a short while, but be sure to return her to me," Travis says to them.

"She said yes?" Tracy asks, smiling wide.

"Yeah, she did. Can you believe it?" Travis says, wrapping his arm around me.

"These girls have some stuff planned for you while I get some things done. We're in for the best day of our life."

Apparently my voice doesn't want to make an appearance at the wedding today because all I can do is stand there grinning from ear to ear.

Kissing me, he whispers, "I love you, Sweets." Then he pulls away and walks back inside the Love Shack while looking back at me, winking.

"Come on girl, we got a wedding to get you ready for," Tracy says, grabbing my hand. We start walking down the sidewalk and I have no idea where we're headed.

"Where are we going?"

"A local salon offered to take care of us," Tracy says.

Apparently I've found my voice because I stop dead in my tracks and exclaim, "I'M GETTING MARRIED TODAY!"

The girls laugh.

"To Travis," Laura adds.

We walk into a small salon about a half a block away. We're greeted by the owner, who directs each of us to sit in a chair.

Tracy stands behind me. "I'm doing your hair today," she says enthusiastically.

"I can't believe this. How long have you guys known?"

Julie laughs. "I've only known for three days."

"Travis and Mom started planning a week ago," Marla confesses.

I stare at her in shock. "Mom helped to plan it? And wait, did you say it's only been a week?"

"Mom had a big part in planning all of today. Not to mention, she's paying for it too. It's beautiful to watch those two together. Wait until you see what they have in store for you."

My mom, on her death bed, helped to plan this and paid for it. That's admirable.

I try to get more information from the girls, but none of them are willing to offer up any details of the day. After a while, Tracy spins me around in the chair and hands me a mirror. I look into it at the most magnificent hair. She twisted my hair to the back of my head in a figure eight, and directly in the center lays a single sunflower. It's beautiful.

We eat lunch that Travis arranged to have delivered, and then we get our nails done. All of us are so giddy with excitement that we can barely contain ourselves. After our nails are buffed and polished, the owner directs us to a back room.

My heart stops the instant I walk through the door. There hangs a white dress that is both simple and elegant. It's a mid-calf, chiffon dress with spaghetti straps, and a band of beads and stones wrap around the waist. It couldn't be a more perfect dress for a beach wedding.

"Travis picked it out," Marla says.

"It's perfect."

I take it in my hands and can't wait a moment longer to put it on. Marla helps me to slip into it. "You're gorgeous. But I have two more things for you." She reaches over and grabs a small box.

Opening it, she takes out a pearl necklace and earrings. "You need something old, something new, and something blue. Your dress is the something new. This is the something old. It's Mom's pearl necklace and earrings that she wore on her wedding day." She puts it around my neck and I put the earrings on.

Marla reaches over and grabs a small bag. "You need something blue and Travis took care of that. As your sister, I don't really want to look inside," she jokes.

She hands the bag to me and I reach in, pulling out light blue lace thong underwear. I laugh.

"I love that boy."

I return from the restroom and the rest of the girls are in their dresses. They're wearing pale yellow, strapless chiffon dresses that go down to their knees.

"Wow Amy, you look sensational," Laura says.

"So do you guys."

"Travis picked out the dresses," Tracy responds. "He's got quite the taste."

"That's my brother," Marla quips.

"Thank you guys for being here with me today," I say, feeling emotional, seeing them dressed up.

"You couldn't keep me away even if you tried," Tracy remarks.

"I love you guys."

Marla's phone rings, and she answers it, walking out of the room. Moments later, she returns nodding. "Are we ready?" My heart starts doing somersaults in my chest as a result of both nerves and excitement.

After thanking the salon owner, we head outside to find Travis' Cadillac awaiting us, with Drew behind the wheel. When he gets out of the car, I see he's dressed in

DECEPTION

tan linen pants and a white linen, button-down shirt. He looks dapper.

"I hear that we have a wedding to get to," he says, walking up to me and kissing my cheek. "You look beautiful," he remarks.

I hug him. "Thanks. You look great yourself."

"Can you believe it? I'm finally getting married," I say, with excitement bursting out of me.

"Finally," he says, laughing.

We get into the car and Drew drives us to the Love Shack. Pulling up to the front, I notice that there are a lot of cars here. Butterflies have returned to my stomach—the same ones that I thought had hit the road long ago.

"Are you ready?" Drew asks, grabbing my hand.

"I'm ready to go marry my man."

After getting out of the car, the girls kiss me on the cheek and march inside. Drew holds my hand while we wait until the girls are gone.

"I guess it's our turn. Don't be nervous, Sis," he says, seeing my anxious expression. "I can't wait for Travis to see you," he adds, smiling.

Walking to the front door, he opens it and we walk inside. The place looks as awe-inspiring as it did this morning. When we approach the front of the bar, I look out at the sea of people on the patio and the beach—lots of people. The butterflies start fluttering so much more than they have ever.

Drew nods to a disc jockey who fidgets with some knobs causing the music to begin. When I listen closely, I note that it's not the traditional wedding march song; I recognize that it's Beautiful in White.

Drew wraps my hand around his arm. "Ready?" he asks. I nod.

We walk out onto the patio, and I become choked up at the sight that awaits me at the end of the aisle. Travis is standing there in tan linen pants and a white linen button-down shirt that matches Drew's, and he looks incredible. Amanda is standing by his side in a light-yellow strapless chiffon dress that resembles the rest of the girls' dresses, and my mom is sitting in a wheelchair on the other side of him. The smile on her face lights up the moment her eyes catch mine.

Tears stream down my face, and the more I attempt to stop them, the more they flow. The sight of the three of them up there stops my breathing and I can barely walk. Drew squeezes my hand in recognition.

We make our way halfway down the aisle, and Travis begins to walk in our direction. When he gets to us he swipes a tear from my cheek.

"I couldn't watch you any longer. You are absolutely breathtaking," he says, leaning in. Even

DECEPTION

bigger tears fall from my eyes when he takes my other hand in his, and the three of us continue to walk to the front.

Drew kisses me on the cheek and whispers, "I love you, Sis."

He hugs Travis before taking a seat in the front row.

I stroll over to my mom and hug her. "I love you so much, Mom. Thank you." Looking at me through tear-stained eyes, she nods and squeezes my hand.

I go over to Amanda and give her a hug, and her smile reaches her eyes. Returning to my gorgeous fiancé who's standing in the center, he grabs my hands in his while I position myself in front of him.

A woman appears next to us and begins the ceremony. "Dearly beloved, we are gathered here today in the presence of these witnesses, to join Amy Silver and Travis Cashman in matrimony, which is commended to be honorable among all men. And therefore, is not by any to be entered into unadvisedly or lightly, but reverently, discreetly, advisedly and solemnly. These two persons present now come to be joined. If any person can show just cause why they may not be joined together, let them speak now or forever hold their peace."

The guests cheer and whistle, bringing Travis and I to laughter. Travis raises his hand in a stance of victory, his face lighting up with a gorgeous smile.

The woman continues. "I believe Travis has prepared some vows," she says, motioning to Travis.

He looks at me, attentively. "Many people spend their lives searching for their soul mate—their one true love. Some people are lucky to find the person they can truly call the better half of themselves, while others spend the rest of their lives searching and never finding. I'm happy to count myself among the lucky ones, because I found you. I love you, Sweets. I know that you're the only one for me—my one true love. I'm happy and I'm grateful that you came into my life, that where others have spent their entire lives looking for the one, I didn't have to search for long. I found you at the age of fifteen, and now that I have you back, I will never let you go. I promise that I shall hold you and cherish you and give you my heart for eternity. One night, not so long ago, I mentioned that Amanda was the second-best thing to happen to me. I never mentioned what my first was. It's you."

I swallow hard. His words spoke directly to my soul.

Without redirecting his gaze, the woman asks if I have vows I would like to share. I nod, while exhaling.

DECEPTION

"I haven't had time to prepare what I would like to say, so I'm going to let my heart do the talking. I love you, not only for what you are, but for what I am when I'm with you. I love you, not only for what you have made of yourself, but for what you are making of me. I love you, for the part of me that you bring out. I love you, because you've done more than any other could have done to make me good, and more than any fate could have done to make me happy. You have done it without a touch, without a word, without a sign. You've done it by being yourself. You taught me true love seventeen years ago. I lost you along the way, but now that I got you back, I'm finally whole again. It is you and me, until eternity."

Tears stream from Travis' eyes, and I reach over and wipe them. He closes his eyes in response.

The woman continues. "Who supports this couple in their marriage?"

Drew and Marla stand. They go to my mom's side and wheel her chair next to us. My mom raises her hand in the air.

I mouth, "I love you," when she looks over at me.

"And who has the rings?" the woman asks.

Amanda steps forward.

The woman looks at Travis. "Repeat after me," she requests. "I, Travis, give you, Amy, this ring as an eternal symbol of my love and commitment to you."

After repeating the phrase, he extends his hand to mine, sliding the wedding band on. He brings my hand up to his mouth, kissing it.

"Amy, repeat after me," the woman then says. "I, Amy, give you, Travis, this ring as an eternal symbol of my love and commitment to you." I repeat, and then take the ring from Amanda and slide it on Travis' finger. I look up at him with excitement.

"By the power vested in me, by the State of California, I now pronounce you husband and wife. Now, Travis, kiss your bride."

He doesn't wait a moment longer. He grabs my face in his hands and kisses me passionately. All the worry and stress of the world melts right out of me.

"I present to you, Mr. and Mrs. Travis Cashman," the woman announces.

The guests jump out of their seats and cheer.

"I'm your wife," I say, no longer able to contain myself.

"Finally."

With Amanda on one side and Travis on the other, I wheel my mom back down the aisle, while our family and friends follow behind.

DECEPTION

We spend the rest of the afternoon, and into the evening, arm-in-arm talking with guests, drinking and eating, and basking in the pure glory that is Mr. and Mrs. Cashman.

A while later, the photographer asks to take a few pictures. Travis pulls me onto the beach when he sees that the sun is about to set.

"You look incredible," he says, wrapping his arms around me and pulling me in.

"You, my husband, look simply delicious in this outfit," I whisper, drawing his mouth to mine. We get lost in our kiss as the sun goes down.

We're interrupted when Drew taps Travis on the shoulder. "It's time," he announces.

I narrow my eyes, looking at Travis. He smirks.

We stroll back into the Love Shack, and he brings me onto the dance floor.

Walking over to the DJ, he grabs a microphone. "I know that your dad isn't here for you to have your father daughter dance, but your mom wants to have a mother daughter dance instead. She's picked this song especially for you."

My mom is up on her feet, being assisted, walking to me. I completely lose it, again. The song My Wish begins to play, and I take her in my arms and we dance. I hold her tight and press my cheek up to hers. I thank her for being the person that she is, for bringing Travis back to me, and for everything that she's done for me in my life. She doesn't speak—she can't speak—but the hold that she has on me and the look in her eyes is enough for me to know that this is exactly how she wanted her life to end.

The song ends, and Drew and Marla's husband, Greg, return with her wheelchair. She sits but motions to Drew. He walks over to the DJ and grabs the microphone. "Travis, your parents couldn't be here, and Mom wanted you to have your mother son dance so it's now your turn."

Travis stands frozen with his mouth agape, speechless. My mom stands back up out of her chair with assistance, and Travis rushes to her.

The song Kind and Generous begins to play, and Travis takes her in his arms and they glide across the dance floor. Travis holds her close while whispering in her ear. Large tears stream down both of their faces. I'm left without words, admiring the beauty in front me.

DECEPTION

The song ends, and they help my mom back to her chair and return her to the side of the dance floor. I go and hug her and wipe the tears from her face.

"Let's lighten things up a bit," Drew says in the microphone. Travis goes to his side and they both have a sly look on their faces.

Travis grabs the microphone. "Bear with us. We were a bit bored today waiting for the girls to get ready, so we've only had a few hours to practice this. But here goes nothing." The song Bringing Sexy Back starts to play.

They stand in the middle of the dance floor and strut around. The guests erupt in applause and whistles. Slowly kicking off their shoes, they toss them to the side. Everyone starts chanting, "Take it off." They strut around a bit more in an attempt to look seductive and, despite what everyone else is thinking, Travis is pulling it off quite well. They then start unbuttoning their shirts in sync with each other, and all of a sudden the dance floor fills up with more guys as they all join in. I keep my eyes locked on Travis. When they throw their shirts toward us, all the women rush to grab them as they fall, acting overly excited when they catch them. They put their hands on the buttons of their pants, slowly unbuttoning them while the song ends. The women all chant, "Booooo." Travis looks adorable with his playful smile, but he also looks damn hot in his linen pants.

He walks in my direction and I run to him, jumping up and wrapping my legs around him, kissing him. The guests erupt in cheers and clink silverware to their glasses.

Before I can say anything, he lowers me back down when he hears the song change. He grabs his shirt and puts it on, leaving it unbuttoned. He takes my hand in his and wraps his other arm around me, pulling me in.

"This song is for you," he whispers.

The DJ announces that it's our first dance, while the song At Last begins to play. I pull him close and rest my cheek against his, and he sings into my ear. If this is what heaven feels like, please take me now. This man is so incredible, and I'm certain that I'm the luckiest woman on the planet.

The song ends and Travis twirls his finger in the air to the DJ.

The song begins again, and we continue to dance while he sings to me. The room is so silent that you can hear a pin drop. Everyone stands around, watching us. My heart is calm—it's content.

DECEPTION

We spend the next few hours dancing and chatting with guests. The DJ announces that everyone is to go outside on the beach. I look at Travis and he winks.

He leads me outside, just as a display of the most beautiful fireworks bursts into the sky.

"You did this?" I ask, wide-eyed. He smiles his most stunning smile. I lay my head on his shoulder and we enjoy the light show.

After the fireworks are finished, Drew lets us know that Mom is tired, and she's requested that he take her home.

We go on the patio where she's sitting and I hug her. "Thank you so much for today. It was simply magical."

She puts her hand over her heart and nods.

Travis leans down and hugs her, while whispering something in her ear.

"I'll see you tomorrow," I say. She kisses my cheek.

Drew wheels her out. Other guests begin to leave as well, and Amanda's grandparents come to pick her up.

We take to the dance floor some more. Travis leans in and whispers, "I have one more surprise for you." I look up excitedly at him. "Come, let's go. The guests won't even know we've gone," he says, giving a wave to a few friends as we walk to the door.

We get in his Cadillac, and I cuddle in close. Twenty minutes later, we pull into the driveway of his new house. He doesn't say anything—he simply comes to my side of the car and takes my hand helping me out. He scoops me up into his arms, and I yelp in response.

The pathway and porch are lit up with a path of candles. After strolling up the stone pathway and onto the porch, he pushes the front door open to a path of candles leading up the stairway. Kicking the door closed behind him, he climbs up the stairs while kissing me.

We reach the bedroom door, and he pushes it open. I gasp at the view. In the bedroom sits a lone king-sized bed, draped in white silk sheets. Candles and sunflowers illuminate the room in a warm glow.

"I couldn't wait until we moved in to see how we like this bedroom," he says, laying me on the bed. "And I really couldn't take seeing you in that dress much longer. I'm anxious to see those blue underwear, Mrs. Cashman," he says, lowering himself on top of me.

I put my hand up to his chest, pushing him back. "No, Mr. Cashman," I whisper, raising an eyebrow.

He narrows his seductively gray eyes in confusion and stands.

DECEPTION

Leaning back on my elbows, I look up at him with lust.

"Your wife first needs to see more of that striptease you started on the dance floor."

epilogue

My mom passed away three days after the wedding. She slipped into sleep and never awoke. She was comfortable and content, with her family surrounding her when she joined my dad—her true love. Her memorial service was two days later. She wanted a small gathering of her close family. The service was somber but beautiful. My aunt Jackie—her sister—spoke about her life and the love that she had for her family. My mom had already made arrangements for everything. She never wanted to bother her kids with any of the matters surrounding her death. After her memorial, my aunt handed me, Drew, and Marla a letter that my mom had written while she was on her death bed. That gesture, along with my wedding that she had a firsthand role in planning, made me realize that while others may have seen her as dying—it being her last days here on earth—she saw it as an opportunity to simply continue caring for her family as she always did. I always admired my mom for the unconditional love that she had, and the many sacrifices she made throughout her life for us. She was a woman with so much grace. On the day she died, she looked happy. She gave me the greatest gift I will ever receive, and I could never repay her for it. But seeing how happy she was on my wedding day, confirmed to me that it wasn't only a gift for me but it was one for her as well. There is no denying the love that she had for Travis, and he for her. And the thought that she got to spend a year with him before she passed makes my heart happy. While I thought every passing day would get easier without her, instead, I miss her more every day. I don't think anything could fill the void I have in my heart for her, and her memories only fill a small part of it. She left each of her children a sizable amount of money. I still haven't gotten myself to do anything with mine. I feel like she already did and paid for so much that it doesn't feel right to use it, so I've tucked mine away for a rainy day. I feel her with me every day—I wake up thinking about her and catch myself in thought during the day. And then I end my day thanking her for bringing my soul mate back to me. I even wake up many nights looking at the clock, to find that it's three-thirty-six—the time that she passed away. I find great comfort in knowing that she's watching over me.

A week later, I put my house on the market and accepted an offer that was well below market value. I felt content in shedding myself of the place that I once called home, but never really felt at home in. I took the money that I made from the sale and paid for Amanda's plastic surgery over the summer and put the rest in an account for her future. I got great joy in putting that money toward helping her—the same money that I once felt was dirty as a result of my dad's outrageous plan. Travis was right, Amanda is such a beautiful young lady inside and out. She has welcomed me so openly, and even recently has called me Mom. I could never replace her mom but knowing that she's developed a love for me so great that she feels like I help fill the void—if even a little—is both overwhelming and wonderful. We're lucky to have her in our life.

Around the same time, I decided to accept the teaching position at the law school. I made Laura and Matthew partners at the firm and turned over complete management to them. I agreed to stay on consulting, but I've enjoyed spending my days in the classroom instead. While I do believe that my dad had a big influence on my decision to pursue law, I'm now also certain that it is what I feel most comfortable doing. I enjoy the sense of accomplishment I get every day, when I'm standing at the front of the class, molding the minds of future lawyers. I see the desire and drive that I once had in every one of the students, and it's refreshing. Teaching has also afforded me more flexibility, and as a result I've been spending a lot of time at the Love Shack. I often take my laptop and work from there. It's still my favorite place to be—that is, besides in Travis' arms. Travis and I have been able to spend a lot of time together, it's been remarkable.

While moving out of the law firm, we made a significant discovery. Upon moving the desk out of my office, a stack of envelopes, bound by elastic, were found tucked away behind a drawer. The envelopes contained the letters that Travis had written to me the weeks following our breakup. I'm certain my dad had forgotten he had placed them there. Each envelope was still sealed, still unread. Travis and I have spent many nights reading them in bed together. There is no denying the love that he's always had for me. And had I received those letters seventeen years ago, I would have seen that he could have never cheated on me. His words glide across the paper and are filled with so much emotion.

Last week Laura told me that her sister gave birth to a baby boy, and apparently Rich has become quite the happy dad. I can't say that I'm not happy for him. As much as I want to harbor ill feelings toward him for the rest of my life, I can't. I'll never forgive him for agreeing to what he did with my dad, but if Sarah is the one that he fell in love with, then how could I be angry with him over that. If my life's journey has taught me anything, it's that we don't get to choose who we fall in love with, our hearts do that for us. I wish them nothing but a good life and happy family.

Rich isn't the only one with a growing family. Two weeks after the wedding, Travis and I decided to stop my birth control and to start trying to have a baby. Well, apparently our tries worked, because four weeks—to the day—after we made that decision, I was staring at two blue lines on a pregnancy test. Upon finding out, Travis went into full daddy mode. His excitement is contagious. We did have a bit of a surprise at our ultrasound in August, when the technician revealed that there were two heartbeats. While it took me a great deal of time to get over that shock, it never seemed to break Travis' stride. It possibly even sparked it that much more. I guess the plans of getting married and having three kids, like we had when we were younger, is going to become a reality quite soon. The look on Amanda's face when we told her was priceless. She couldn't contain her excitement, and she's joined Travis in preparing the nursery. The thought of having two lives growing inside of me, as a result of the love between Travis and I, is beautiful. I'm looking forward to sharing the experience of raising a family with my one true love. It all feels right. Being pregnant and losing my mom has made me realize what really matters in life, so I've decided to take a year off from teaching once the babies are born. Who knows, I may decide to take more time off afterward. I'm now starting to understand the desire and need that my mom had to care for her family. Travis, Amanda, the babies growing in my belly, and my siblings—there's nothing else that matters more to me in this world.

This is our love story, and I couldn't have dreamt up a better ending. While we were certainly presented with an obstacle, love won out in the end. It always will.

My mom's hand-written letter to me:

My beautiful baby girl,

If you're reading this that means that I'm now with your dad. But my heart will be with you forever. I will be there during your greatest accomplishments and your darkest days. Please remember the things that I've taught you and the ones that you've taught me. I've always admired you. You have always taken pride in the things that you've done. I know that life has presented you with more than your share of challenges, but please remember to never get angry at the small things and that most people are good. But most importantly, when in doubt, always lean on the side of love. Life means so much, but people mean so much more.

I will miss you just as much as you miss me. But knowing that you're now in the arms of your true love, I know that you'll be fine. Travis is a man unlike any other and you're fortunate

DECEPTION

to have him back in your life, but he's also equally as fortunate to have you. I'm certain that if your dad would have had the chance to experience the two of you together as I have, he would have never gone to the lengths that he did to keep you two apart. Your love for each other radiates. There's nothing more a mom could ask for.

Always remember that my love for you will never die,

Your mom